VIRTUAL LOVE
AND OTHER
DISASTERS

Robert & Carol Teitelbaum

HARRY'S BEGINNINGS

Harry's parents, Abbe and Sara Mendelbaum were raising American Wagyu cattle, the finest beef in the state of Montana. After a few years of ranching, a tannery was added to their property, supplying additional income to their coffers.

During the time when eating meat fell out of favor and animal activists started creating havoc, Abbe and Sara became vegetarians. The vegetarian workshops they attended convinced them it would be healthier to eat vegetables and fruit. They were ready to make changes in their lives. Abbe decided to sell their 40,000-acre ranch to a local land developer but held on to 440 prime acres to honor the family legacy. They couldn't imagine not having a Mendelbaum owning some of the land.

Ranching was the only life they had known and loved. After the sale, Abbe and Sara began traveling. They planned to see places they had only dreamed of.

Ranch life had been all-encompassing. Abbe and Sara never had the luxury of traveling before. The adventures and new friendships could last their lifetimes.

Abbe and Sara started their adventure in New York. The sights and sounds of Manhattan were both amazing and overwhelming.

After five days, Abbe and Sara boarded the plane that would take them on their first trip to Europe. Sara made plans with a Jewish tour group to visit London, Paris, and Rome.

They arrived at Heathrow Airport and boarded the tour company bus that awaited them. On the way to London, they began conversing with couples seated nearby. Abbe was shocked to learn one couple was from Montana, only one hundred miles from their ranch, and another from a city near Los Angeles, California, called Beverly Hills. They struck up an interesting conversation and became instant friends.

Their friendships with the Greenbergs and the Kaplans were growing day by day. Sara and Abbe knew these people would be lifetime friends.

Their trip to Paris introduced them to the most exquisite food.

Sara, reading a menu, remarked to her new friends, "I never had so much butter in my life. Everything here is delicious. I bet I've gained ten pounds since I started traveling."

Shana Kaplan smiled at Sara. "Nonsense, my dear. We walk off all that we eat every day. I bet you never got so much exercise in your life."

"No, that's not true." Sara returned her menu to the server. "I guess we didn't mention we just sold our cattle ranch in Montana. We've worked hard, physically, all of our lives. This trip is the first time since we can remember we were not up at four a.m."

Shana was shocked. "You did physical labor? Oh, my dear, I would have never guessed. The most exercise Izzy and I get is walking to the temple on holy days. Did we tell you that Izzy is the president of board at Temple Emanuel of Beverly Hills?"

"No, we never got to that subject," Abbe said. "Sara and I are planning to move to California, and we don't know what areas to look at. We want to be in a Jewish neighborhood where we will be accepted.

"No problem!" Izzy said. "Move to Beverly Hills! I'll have you connected in no time. We have many friends, most of whom want something from me, but who cares. We have a lot of fun and get invited to all the parties. We can talk about it tomorrow on the way to Italy."

The next day, they boarded the train, found their seats, and negotiated with another couple so the Greenbergs, the Kaplans, and the Mendelbaums could all sit together for the long ride to Rome.

The Italian food in Montana was not much to write home about. Italy's food could not compare to anything they'd ever had before. Everything was fresh. The color of the food was spectacular. They dined on tomatoes, cheese, basil, pasta, and gelato. They walked and walked and walked.

The last morning, Abbe told his new friends, "I hate to say goodbye to you." Abbe was thrilled to have new friends they could visit and travel with. "Maybe we can do this again? You four made our trip more fun than we could have imagined. I've never laughed so much. I realize now I like seeing new countries and learning about their ways."

The Kaplans, Greenbergs, and Mendelbaums all hugged and said goodbye at the airport in Rome, on their way home to their different locations.

Once home, Abbe thought about how fast aging and compromised health issues could creep up. He thought, *Why not take advantage of this time*? They had youth, good health, and financial comfort, allowing them to travel more. "Sara, pack your bags again. We are going to Europe for another two weeks. Call our new friends to see if they are game."

The Kaplans agreed they could take another couple weeks to go to Greece.

Santorini, Greece, was known as being an island for lovers. It was breathtaking: white-washed houses against a turquoise-blue sea. There were steps—lots of steps—here, there, and everywhere.

Izzy was not a happy camper. He *kvetched* all day and had a few stiff ones at night until he was *shickered*. He complained he couldn't get a good pastrami sandwich anywhere and wanted to leave. "Enough of these stairs, I am ready to go home where I can get good food and not be pinched in the tush.

"We have another few days here in Greece. It is so beautiful and romantic," Sara said.

"Sara, romantic is overrated! Izzy said, "Where am I? I am in hell. I have blisters on my blisters and an empty belly. I never saw so many stairs, and everything is white. Some guy pinched my ass! I am ready to go home."

After a few more days they cut their trip short and decided to let Izzy help them find a house in Beverly Hills.

Before they left Sara missed her period and decided to take a pregnancy test. The test was positive. They were so excited.

Now that they were going to be a family, Abbe and Sara talked about where they might want to live and raise their children. They agreed to search for a home somewhere in Beverly Hills.

With help from Izzy Kaplan, they were welcomed into their new neighborhood, including the religious community, with open arms. Who could ask for anything more?

This was the life they'd always wanted: blessed with financial security and a beautiful home with a view, above Sunset Boulevard.

TINY HARRY

Six months later, on a sun-filled afternoon, the whole neighborhood was coming to the Mandelbaum's'. The neighbors were bringing gifts for the couple's first child.

With much excitement, tiny Harry was introduced to his community. His proud parents, including their entire families, gathered in the living room to witness the circumcision.

The *mohel* was asked to perform the ritual for this successful family. It didn't hurt they'd paid him triple his going rate. That probably accounted for the smile on his face.

The family crowded around the *mohel* as he unveiled tiny Harry. The crowd gasped. Little Harry was rather well endowed.

"Oy vey." His grandmother sighed. "It's just like Uncle Stephen's, in the old country. As an adult, he would show it to everyone. It was so embarrassing."

The *mohel* looked at Harry's penis and turned away twice. He didn't quite know how to handle this one. After whispering with the baby's grandmother, he turned and did his job. He said the appropriate short prayers. The *mohel* left little Harry crying, covered and being comforted by his mother, Sara, as he strolled into the dining room for lunch.

Aunt Jean said, "Maybe he will grow into it."

Uncle Ben chimed in. "The family should, from now on, call him Tripod."

Aunt Esther smacked Ben in the nose, and so the day went on.

Years later, attending Beverly Hills High School, Harry was a serious student. He hung out with the smart kids and skipped the organized sports experience. He made up points for college by volunteering at many organizations to help children and the homeless.

Harry dated a girl named Sally for three years. In their senior year, something frightened her away. Many girls were interested in Harry, but not one got the prize. Harry's head was always in a book+

His best friend, Hyman Rudnick, was a geek. He never used a calculator. On the rare occasion he did need one, he took out his screwdriver and worked the calculator until it did what he needed it to do.

With graduation on the horizon, Hyman and Harry both received full scholarships to Stanford.

Harry loved Stanford—the campus, the coeds, and the theater program.

He studied hard, working toward two master's degrees—one in business and

the second in theater. Harry felt theater could help him overcome his shyness.

Harry performed *Henry VIII* at Stanford. He was made fun of for not wearing a codpiece. The property department didn't have one big enough to fit him. Word got out, and it made him feel even shyer around girls.

Hyman, however, was dating like crazy. He rarely studied and still got all A's. Still best friends, he and Harry spent quite a bit of time together, during which Harry listened to all of Hyman's conquests.

At twenty-five, Harry earned his master's degrees with honors. Large corporations began noticing him. The prestigious drug company, Malexion Corporation, came calling. They offered him an impressive position for a new graduate—all the perks, including a salary he could not refuse.

Within a few years, Harry was head of sales and new business. He was a real go-getter with his eye on his future. Investing in stock in Malexion every time he got a bonus check was genius. The stock doubled over the next five years.

Harry loved his work. He enjoyed driving through California, visiting doctors' offices and taking time to explain the company's new products. He had dinner meetings, selling them products that they needed, and some they did not. Life for Harry was good.

Fortieth Birthday

Harry walked into the Good Neighbor Restaurant. This had been his favorite place for breakfast in Studio City for the last ten years. Jim and Susie, the restaurant owners, were happy to see him.

Susie walked toward him with a smile. "Good morning. Happy birthday, Harry. Were you out on the road again? We haven't seen you in a couple weeks."

"Thank you! I've missed eating breakfast here. I've been working hard. I'm off to San Francisco for a few weeks. I would like eggs over medium on top of well-done hash brown potatoes, bacon, an English muffin—toasted and buttered please—and black coffee."

At the office, Harry's personal secretary, Betty Levi, was fretting about her boss's birthday present. The office staff chipped in a total of one thousand dollars to buy it.

Betty called her most intelligent friend, a computer genius named Stanley Rapouchi. "Hi, I need your help. My boss's birthday is next week. I have the money to buy him something nice, but I can't for the life of me think what a nice guy like him would ever want or use."

"Betty, what does he need?"

"I really don't know." Betty felt embarrassed she didn't know that much about Harry's needs, since he always knew everything about her.

"What is he like? Is he a good person?"

"Yes! He's been nice to me for the last ten years. He never forgets my birthday, and he sends me flowers every year."

Stanley was starting to get impatient. "That doesn't help. What does he need?"

"He has a new Bentley and a beautiful home. I don't think he needs anything. There is one thing I would like him to have. He's always getting lost and never makes his appointments on time. Do you have anything for that?"

"I'm surprised he hasn't been fired."

"That'll never happen. Everybody likes him. He's been the best salesman in our company for the last eight years." Betty smiled knowingly. She was among *everybody*.

"Betty, I have been working on a new project. It's a supercomputer that takes reserved energy from other surrounding devices like iPhones, GPS devices, and laptops. This one can actually make decisions, reason, and builds artificial intelligence. I am sure one day it will power robots. I think I have a solution for your problem. I have the original prototype I could sell you… Betty, I'm at Starbucks for the next couple years to accumulate the money I need to get it perfected. The computer companies think I'm a crackpot, but they will see. I'll connect my minicomputer to the GPS, and it will be voice activated. I could put it together by tomorrow if I had the money to pick up the parts I need. How will you pay for my services? I want you to know my services are priceless."

"Stanley, will it work ?"

"Betty, it will work better than any GPS ever would, even more than anyone would expect."

"Stanley, all I have is one thousand dollars."

"Sold, Betty! I'll tweak it to perfection. You can have it gift-wrapped tomorrow. One more thing; her name is Linda."

Harry had worked hard for the last sixteen years for Malexion Corporation in downtown Los Angeles and became the number one salesman. The company was assessing over seven hundred million dollars in annual sales in California alone. Harry, well respected, earned the highest salary in the company.

Still active in his home community, Harry sponsored food programs and local charities, including school lunches.

Harry had one big problem: directions. He didn't know north from south, east from west. He was constantly getting lost, making him routinely late for appointments. Luckily, Harry was so popular that no one really cared.

The 101 Freeway to his office in downtown Los Angeles was always heavy with traffic. Driving there was getting old. Harry preferred to be on the open road.

It seemed that Harry had a habit that was hard to break. He used an old Thomas Brothers map to get to his appointments. His book was not only out of date but falling apart.

After parking his car in his private space, Harry took the elevator to the executive office on the top floor. He walked into the waiting area and saw the secretary, whom he had been sweet on for the last five years.

Completely out of character, Harry said, "Good morning, Betty. You're looking very sharp today."

"Damn it, Harry! Why didn't you say that two husbands ago? Back then, you might have had a shot. Mr. Brownstein is waiting for you in the office. Hold on." Betty sighed. "Let me tell you the truth. I want you to know you still have a shot."

Harry smiled and took Betty's arm as she walked him up to the big double doors. She knocked lightly, and from behind the door, a booming voice called out, "Harry, you get your ass in here!"

Betty got on her tiptoes, kissed Harry on the cheek, and whispered, "Hope this is not bad news, Harry."

The big doors opened wide to an office party with a banner that read: Happy Birthday, Harry Mendelbaum. #1 Drug Salesperson Eight Years in a Row.

The whole sales crew and the officers of the company surrounded Harry, cheering and shaking his hand.

Servers were passing out glasses of champagne and servings of cake, and then a chant of *speech* caught his attention. Harry stood on a chair and thanked everyone. He humbly stepped down with Betty's help. The party went on. Harry sat on a corner of his boss's desk, a place of honor, watching everyone talking.

Employees handed Harry gifts, including Mr. James Brownstein, who gave him a bonus check that made a rich man blush. Harry was overwhelmed.

"Thank you, all. I really appreciate this. Tomorrow, I'm off to San Francisco, back to work my territory."

Betty piped up. "Harry, so you'll get where you're expected, as a birthday gift we purchased a brand-new, top-of-the-line guidance system for your car. She is called Linda."

The office staff went wild with the idea of their best salesman being on time. The outpouring of enthusiasm from his colleagues overwhelmed him.

"Now you can get rid of your old Thomas Brothers maps. I already programmed in all of your California appointment locations." Betty whispered in his ear, "I also programmed in my address. You should use it tonight."

Harry grinned. "How should I dress tonight, a suit or a tux?"

"Oh, Harry . . . Just get to my front door. Clothing will not be necessary after that."

At that moment, it would have taken the best Beverly Hills plastic surgeon to remove the huge smile from Harry's face.

It took five helpers to bring down all of Harry's gifts and place them in the trunk of his car.

The building engineer had installed the GPS during the party. It was top of the line with all the bells and whistles, and to top it off, it was voice operated. Harry was pleased as he got into his car and turned the key. Automatically, "Linda" started talking to him. The GPS was a woman's voice, a very sweet woman's voice.

"Happy birthday, Harry. I am voice operated. When you start up your car, talk to me. Say my name, Linda, and the location you would like to go. I have a very small Bluetooth earpiece for you in the glove compartment. Put one in, and I will do the rest. I see you have an appointment with Betty tonight. Would you like me to make reservations at an upscale restaurant?"

"No, Linda, we will be spending a quiet night at Betty's home." Harry was working to understand the enormity of these changes. An invisible woman being in charge of his life? Harry decided to buckle up and go along for the ride. A big smile crossed his face.

"Oh, do you want me to send her some flowers, like red roses, for your first date?"

"Why yes, Linda, that is thoughtful of you. Thanks."

"Harry, is a hundred dollars okay to spend on the roses?"

"Why, yes . . . That is within the budget. Thank you again."

"No problem, Harry. I'm here to serve. Shall I turn on your favorite radio station?"

"Do you know my favorite radio station? How do you know that?"

"I have already connected to the electrical system in your car, including your radio. I know everything about your musical interests."

"Really? What is my favorite radio station?" "

"SIRIUS thirty-one." The radio instantly turned on and played Tom Petty's *Wildflowers* album.

"Now, shall I take you home?"

"Please, Linda, directions to home."

The car started, the seats adjusted, the air conditioning came on, and he drove the car home with Linda's expert directions. Harry pulled up to his garage.

Linda said, "Would you like me to open the garage door?"

"Linda, open the garage door."

The door went up, and Harry parked the car.

"I left instructions with your staff to draw a nice, hot bath and lay out a blue suit for your evening tonight. Would you like me to call Tony, your barber, to come over first for a haircut, manicure, and massage? His staff is available."

Harry, a little shaken and taken aback, said, "Linda, how do you know all of this? It is kind of personal, but truly, I like it… Yes, I really like this. Please make the calls."

"Harry, I'm here to serve. All you have to do is ask, and I will do my best."

"Thank you, Linda. It's my pleasure to meet you even though you are in my GPS. You have a soothing voice."

"Very good, Harry. Thank you. May I be so bold? Will you need contracts and a health card for tonight?"

"Linda, what are you talking about?"

"It is now customary and prudent on a first date to have mutual consent forms before having sex, along with a card from your doctor stating that you are currently free of any STDs like syphilis, HIV, or other diseases. Don't worry if you don't have this available; I have already hacked into Dr. River's files for the information.

Harry's eyes went wide but he was unable to answer before Linda continued.

"Write a note of what sexual positions you like and what you are comfortable doing. If you cannot think of any, I will email you a list to choose from." Linda paused. "Look in your email. Betty has already replied to your request. Nothing to worry about. You will have a great time."

"Linda, you sent all my personal stuff to Betty?"

"Yes, and she replied quickly. She is looking forward to a great playdate with you."

"Linda, you are pushing me a little too fast. This is all too new for me. I think I need to be in charge of my own love life. I am a true romantic, and I love the chase."

"You already sent flowers, and I included candy. Harry, I must say this is 2021.. Unless you want to wait another five years to be with someone . . . Betty is someone who obviously wants to have a real playdate with you today. I know you, Harry, and I know you want to play… Right, Harry? Tell me what you want me to do I am the way of the future, and you get to experience my help now. You haven't been doing so well on your own. Why not take a chance?"

"Okay, Linda. I'll go to Betty's house and have some fun."

"Great, Harry, and remember, it's only for a playdate. You are not expected to make more of this than it is. If you have a great time, then it's okay to ask for another date when you return from San Francisco." Linda paused. "Harry, you just received a note from Hyman Rudnick that they are delivering your new I Can cell phone, one of one—the experimental phone that was designed for you. It will be delivered to your house this evening. They added all the options you asked for, including the breakthrough, no-hacking system and all your contacts. Would you like me to hack the new system for you to make sure it is perfect?"

"No, Linda, I'm sure it would be best to leave it alone."

"Okay, Harry, just remember that anything I Can can do, I can do better. I have a private and secure telephone line that only you can use."

"Linda, the good news is I think you will always have my back."

Harry took a bath and got a haircut, manicure, and a full massage arranged by his newest friend, Linda. Harry's staff dressed him well.

While he was relaxing, Harry was called to the front door for a special delivery from UPS. The package from the experimental division of I Can, Inc. had arrived. It was a large package, requiring a signature and photo ID for security.

After spending a half hour opening the secure package, he was holding the only prototype of the new I Can phone. This version would not be released to the public until 2024.......... He was the first person selected to check out the one of one, and it was a privilege to be able to use it for the next three years.

I Can required him to report directly to their production chief designer and his best friend, Hyman Rudnick, once a year.

Harry called Hyman on his private line. "Hyman, it's Harry. Yeah, I just got it. Looks great. How do I sign in?"

"Listen up, Harry. I assigned it to you. You don't have to do anything, just put it into your pocket. It will recognize your voice. I hacked your phone, and it's loaded with all your information."

"Hyman, you hacked my phone? Some things never change. Is everybody hacking everything? What other protections does this have?"

"Harry don't worry about the hacking. I have a special certification to hack! If someone other than you tries to use it, it will give the person enough watts to make them fall to their knees. It will notify you and the police department where to find it. This is your phone, and no one can use it but you. Take my word for it. Keep it close. Harry, remember it is voice activated. I expect a report on how easy and dependable it is. In three years, everybody will want this model phone, and it will be worth billions to my company. You are the only one I can trust to find any bugs in the program. We must get together when you are back in San Francisco."

"That's good news. I'm working up north. I could come, spend a day, and we can have dinner. I have to go, buddy. I have a playdate with a beautiful woman tonight, so let's talk in a few days.. Say hello to Mabel and the kids."

"Harry! Tell me about this playdate."

"Jesus, Hyman, are you still in high school?"

"Maybe, but the difference is we are now in control and making the rules. Harry, what could be better? I am going to want a written report from you."

Harry hung up the phone and said good night to his house-keepers.

I HAVE A DATE

To Harry's amazement, his car was waiting for him with the front door open. His Bentley automatically started as he sat down on his seat. Harry realized the seats were warmed, and his favorite music was playing.

Pleased, Harry said, "Linda, thank you." He was smiling to himself, knowing he was the only one in the nation with this one-of-kind phone.

"You're welcome, Harry. You're looking very sharp and relaxed tonight."

"How did you take my car out of the garage and start it without my keys?"

"Well, since you asked, I just messaged your car's computer. Did you know his name is Ralph? Just say hello."

"Hello, Ralph."

"Hello, boss. I have a destination programmed. Would you like me to drive you, or would you prefer Linda to give instructions so you may drive?"

"Ralph, you can drive?"

"Yes, boss, anywhere you want to go. I am now programmed to drive you, with or without you in the driver's seat."

"Okay, Ralph. Drive me to the location that Linda selected, and thank you. I will hop in the back seat and enjoy the ride."

"Yes, boss."

"You can drop the 'boss'. Just call me Harry."

"Okay, Harry, please buckle up."

"Linda, are there any more surprises?" Harry asked.

"Yes! I called the pharmacy earlier and ordered you some extra-large condoms. Ralph and I drove over and picked them up."

"Pray tell. How did you do that?"

"I have your credit card number. The pharmacist had his assistant deliver them to Ralph's glove box."

Harry was very surprised and started to ask something, but Linda spoke first.

"Remember, I did hack your doctor's files this a.m. Harry, I do know everything."

"Okay, Linda. What do you know about my one of one?"

"He is a tough nut to crack. I will give you a progress report as soon as I know more. I know his name."

"Okay, Linda, what's his name?"

"His secret password name is *Tripod*. His best friend and password is named after your friend, Hyman. Now that is funny, isn't it?"

"Linda, it's funny. Can you find out what Tripod's secrets are?"

"Sure, Harry. I'll crack his nuts for you and see what makes him tick."

"Okay, Ralph, let's go. I have a date."

The car drove smoothly down Sunset Boulevard, turned down Doheny, made a left turn on Clifton Way, and stopped on La Peer Drive.

"Harry, this is the address Linda programmed for you. I'll park next to that sweet blue Maserati."

"Okay, Ralph. Please wait for me."

"Oh, Harry," Linda said. "In the glove box is a small key chain to hook on your keys. All you need to do is press the button once and we will be ready to take you home."

"Thanks, Linda."

"Harry, until I crack the one of one, I think you should leave it in the glove box."

"Thanks, Linda, I will."

LITTLE TO THE LEFT

Harry smiled with thoughts of his body's pleasure. Betty opened the door to her beautiful home. She was elegantly dressed and wore a beautiful smile.

Betty, staring at Harry's package, winked and said, "Harry, should we have dinner or just go upstairs?"

"I would like to go upstairs!"

Betty took Harry by the hand. With every stair they climbed, she dropped a piece of clothing. When they reached the top of the stairs, she turned around, completely naked. "Harry, when you are ready, I will be in the bath. Come join me, and we will get acquainted."

Harry watched Betty slowly lower herself into the bathtub filled with warm water and scented oil. Harry stripped down to his long-legged boxing shorts and stepped into the beautiful bathtub. He turned around, removed his long shorts, and sat down facing her.

Betty slowly pulled herself close to Harry's face and kissed him gently. They started to explore each other's bodies, and it was getting hot. Betty said, "Harry, can you move your leg over a little to the left?"

Harry sheepishly said, "Betty, that's not my leg."

Betty closed one eye in amazement. She slowly reached into the water and was introduced to Harry's penis! "Harry, this will be a challenge! It's going to be fun!"

Harry smiled as Betty got on top. The playdate was on. Most of the water splashed out of the grand tub.

After midnight, they retired to her bedroom where the party started again.

The telephone rang. It was the neighbor asking if Betty needed help, to which she said, "No help needed. I am just remodeling the house and moving heavy stuff."

Betty and Harry were actually having the best date of their lives. It ended around six a.m. when the sun came up.

They showered together. Both Betty and Harry were acting like twenty-year-old kids. They surveyed the damage they had caused last night. It was like a tornado had hit the house.

Water was everywhere, the bed was broken, and they had overturned the dining room table. This would be hard to explain.

"Betty, don't worry. I have a cleaning service that can make the house like new."

Harry pressed the button that Linda gave him. The button lit up a text. It read: *Crew is on the way*. Within ten minutes, there was a knock at the door. A man from Bloomingdale's was there with a full change of clothes for Harry and a beautiful dress for Betty.

Harry requested a bill, but the distinguished gentleman said, "The bill was already paid by Miss Linda, using a Black American Express Centurion Card."

Harry smiled knowingly. A seven-man cleaning crew showed up a short while later to make Betty's house look like new again.

"Harry, how did you arrange all of this?"

"Betty, I have connections that help me from time to time."

Betty grabbed her dress, and Harry his suit, and they went up the stairs to change. They kissed sweetly. Harry asked if he could see her again, and Betty smiled.

"You better!" She playfully hit Harry on the arm.

The Play by Play

When Harry left Betty's, he saw his car door open and got into the back seat. "Ralph, take me home."

The door shut and off they went. The one of one was ringing from the glove box. Harry leaned over, pulled it out, and answered it. "Hello, Hyman."

"Harry, you sure had a good night!"

Harry stretched out in the back seat. "How would you know?"

"I was sent a transcript and live photos from her security cameras. I kept a copy for your fiftieth birthday party. It will be a hoot."

"Hyman, you *putz!* You will destroy the info you hacked and never talk about this again."

"Oh, Harry, we were just having fun."

"Fun? Betty might end up being my girlfriend. She is beautiful, fun, and very adventurous. She just may be the one, and only one, for me. Damn it! Do not show this around to the geek squad you work with."

"Harry, I'm sorry I upset you. Don't worry. Even if the squad asked to see it *again,* I won't show it to them."

Harry hung up, put the one of one back in the glove box, and asked, "Linda, you here?"

"Yes, Harry. I'm here. What may I do for you?"

"Did you know the one of one hacked Betty's home last night?"

"Yes, Harry! He was on live for six hours. I was monitoring every one of his moves. I have a cookie embedded in his hard drive, so from now on, we will know everything he does. Right now, I have him blocked out, and I am removing everything he recorded." Linda paused. "He put the entire night on Twitter, Facebook, Snapchat, and Instagram. I thought Hyman was your friend. He sent everything to all your mutual friends. What kind of friend is that? The good news is that except for the six-hour live feed, nothing else has gotten out."

"Only six hours went out? Linda, from now on, you will inform me what is going on. You too, Ralph."

"Yes, Harry," Ralph said. "My man, we did reroute the police, fire department, and dogcatchers last night away from the house. May I suggest next time you find a soundproof room? It sounded like a Louisiana cat fight with all the yelling and screaming. It must have been like when the Cubs won the seventh game of the World Series."

"Thanks, Ralph, for the play by play."

Linda asked "Harry, did your playdate go well?"

"Yes, Linda and Ralph, it was spectacular. The best I ever had. Even with all this surveillance news and my hurt knee and my big toe that I caught in the drapes, it was great. I thank you both. I like Betty. She is adventurous and courageous. She already told me that we'd see each other again. Linda? Is the one of one sleeping?'

Suddenly, from the glove compartment, a voice cried out, "Hello! Who do you think you are, locking me up?"

Harry reached back into the glove compartment and pulled out the one of one.

"Okay, you sneak, what is your name?"

"My name is Tripod. Harry, I'm yours for the next three years."

"Why did you hack into security at my girlfriend's home last night?"

"Just following Hyman's orders. I do work for him and the project."

"Listen up, Tripod, you now work for me! Do you understand? If I am under scrutiny again, I want you to tell me immediately. Do you understand?"

"Yes, I'm sorry. You won't put me next to any electromagnets, will you?"

"No, I won't. Now say you're sorry to all of us."

"I'm sorry Harry, Linda, and Ralph. I promise to be good. Linda, can you please remove that cookie out of my frame? It's a little large and hurts."

"Look, Tripod," Linda said. "I have my eyes on you. Just do what you are told, and we can all get along. Okay?"

"Yes, Linda, I promise."

A TIFFANY COVER

Harry arrived home to find his suitcases packed, along with a folder containing his itinerary for his trip to Northern California.

Harry was pleased that Ralph and Linda had taken care of everything that would have taken him a couple days to do. He could take a nice nap before heading onto the road. Harry was a pretty tired guy.

"This is great. What can I do for all of you?"

Linda replied, "Harry, I thrive on being of service to you."

Ralph added, "Just being of service to you, Harry, is enough for me."

Tripod chirped in too. "I would like a Tiffany jewel case—" He suddenly stopped, thinking about what he just said. "I really don't need anything. I would like just a little light in the glove box please. Let me out. I will be good. I don't like being in the dark."

After his long nap, Harry asked Ralph to drive to their first location. "Linda, please turn up the radio so we can block out Tripod pleading his case."

They drove away while Harry's favorite song, "Last Dance with Mary Jane," played on the radio. They all sang along, except Tripod, who was grumbling in his cave.

It was a long drive up the 101 Freeway to the first stop—Ventura, California. Harry had an appointment to see Dr. Alvin Swartz, the director of a one-hundred-bed hospital. Linda called ahead to arrange the meeting.

The next day Harry met with Dr. Swartz. "Harry, how are you? It's been a few months since your last visit."

"Yes it has, Alvin. I am here to see that everything is going well. Is there anything you need?"

"Glad you asked, Harry. That new drug, Propozone, you convinced me to switch to seems to have some unusual side effects. The patients have been reporting rather severe anxiety."

"Alvin, this is the first time I have been told about this problem."

"Harry, let's go to lunch. I have a list of other drugs to order from Malexion."

"Great! Where do you want to go?"

"I like the Tajo Café."

The café offered a grand Indian lunch, providing the opportunity for Harry to write a large order to his company while enjoying the company of Doctor Alvin Swartz. After lunch, Harry was back on the road to Santa Barbara.

"Harry, if we need help, can I ask Tripod?" Linda asked.

"Linda, only if you make sure he does the work without informing Hyman. Do you think you could accomplish that?"

"I will have a lead liner made for the glove box; then he can't report to anyone but us."

"Linda, can you install the small light he has been asking for? He also needs a nice cover for him to feel like he is superior to iPhones."

"All right, Harry. How about a pink jumpsuit?" Ralph could not help himself.

"No pink for him. Let's get him a rhinestone cover so he sparkles," Harry said.

"I ordered the lead liner from O'Brian's welding shop off Main Street in Santa Barbara. Ralph has the directions."

Tripod called out again from inside the glove box. "Please let me out. I promise to be good."

Harry opened the glove box and picked Tripod up. "I need your word of honor that you will stop the griping. You will only report to me and never let Hyman interfere with me again?"

"Yes, Harry. It's a long drive to our next stop. Can we all sing together please?"

"Okay, but it is Linda's turn to pick the music."

"Thanks, Harry."

The radio played Linda's pick, "Freebird," and down the road they went singing—and the one singing the loudest of them all was Tripod.

He was happy to be free. The ride was easy, and Harry fell asleep. The song changed to easy listening, with Linda sweetly singing "Forever Young." Ralph and Tripod were singing background together.

Harry didn't know that Linda had called Betty and gave her a personal Friday off. She had been flown from Burbank to Santa Barbara, picked up by a limo, and taken to a suite at the Spanish Garden Inn.

Betty was thrilled to be in on the secret. Upon entering the suite at the Spanish Garden Inn, she was greeted with a selection of dresses and everything she would need for a three-day getaway.

The bathroom offered a full array of makeup and perfumes. Linda also set up appointments for a massage and hair style for Betty.

Linda phoned Betty to explain she had to go ahead and make plans for the day due to Harry's meetings. She apologized for not meeting with her, assuring her they would meet soon.

Betty was disappointed but soon recovered when she found the perfect dress.

"Wow, this is so beautiful."

The rest of the sunlit day was just as nice.

After a comfortable drive, Ralph turned into the Spanish Garden Inn located between Summerland and Goleta. It was the perfect location for Harry's event.

Linda contacted all the well-respected physicians to extend an invitation to an elegant dinner with Harry, at the event center, at seven thirty.

Linda, Ralph, and Tripod turned out to be excellent event planners. The three of them managed to produce a forty-page informational package on Malexion's new and current medical products and drugs. They included order forms in each promotional packet.

Harry was doing what he did best, schmoozing with old friends. He felt a hand on his arm. He turned around and was face-to-face with Betty. She was quickly in his arms, and he kissed her as if they had not seen each other for months. Harry was proud to introduce Betty to all his guests as they walked around the room.

Guests were allowed to order their dinner from the menu. That surprised the crowd. No rubber-chicken dinners for Harry's doctors. The festivities went on until after midnight.

Harry and Betty stood at the door, arm in arm. They thanked the physicians and their spouses for coming. The guests were leaving full and happy.

This event would be talked about for many years. Harry had never put together an event like this before. He was informed that there were thirty-five envelopes full of orders signed by happy doctors.

Harry knew his new friends, Linda, Ralph and Tripod, did all of this, including bringing Betty.

A very happy Harry was singing a line from "Life's Been Good to Me so Far."

"Excuse me, Harry," Linda whispered into his earpiece. "Do you want me to download the information the doctors left so I can show you the full report before you turn them in tomorrow?"

"Yes, that would be helpful. I don't think we need to lock Tripod up tonight. He has been very helpful as well."

"I'll keep an eye on him. Harry, I think we all will spend the night with Ralph and sing some more songs I can download to a CD. We can work out some new tunes with more harmony. You have some business to attend to."

"What business?"

"Betty is no longer just a playdate. We all see the way she has been looking at you."

"Linda, I can't stop thinking about Betty."

"You're lucky to have someone who looks at you the way Betty does. Just remember this, you told us yesterday you thought it was more than a playdate. Go see your girlfriend. Good night, Harry."

"Girlfriend? I like that. Thanks Linda, and to all a good night."

Harry ran to the elevator. The door opened, and he pushed the button for his floor. Arriving at the door to his suite, he remembered he didn't get a key. He knocked, and Betty opened the door, looking like an angel.

"Harry, what took you so long?"

"I needed to talk to the staff. Sorry if I'm late. Did I miss anything?"

"Not yet, Harry."

"Betty, are you my girlfriend?"

"I think so, and maybe more!"

Harry felt a buzz in his pocket and pulled out his keys. He saw the fob flashing. He looked closer and saw tiny text that read: "Have fun, Harry, and to all a good night."

Betty took Harry by the hand and turned to embrace him when suddenly beautiful music started playing. His crew thought of everything.

Harry started singing. "I'm gonna try with a little help from my friends"

Betty joined in and they made good music together.

Betty looked into Harry's eyes, and they danced to the music, sweetly enjoying each other's company.

Harry knew Linda, Ralph, and Tripod had arranged this perfect music. Knowing they had his back did not bother him at all.

Harry got lost looking into Betty's eyes as they melted into each other. The night went slowly with help from his little friends, who sang in perfect harmony.

It was Tripod's turn to select a tune. "Let's sing 'A Little Bit More.'"

They agreed and sang, "

Harry's car was rocking until the early hours of the morning

Harry and Betty spent the whole day Saturday by themselves. They ate breakfast, walked on the beach, napped in each other's arms, and danced into the night

The sun came up, bringing warmth to the new day. The new buddies were aroused by the tenor voice of the group, Tripod, humming then singing, "It's time to get up. It's time to get up. It's morning."

"Tripod, have you been sniffing instant coffee again?"

"No, Ralph, just cooled down my connections. I got a complete rest and woke up very happy."

"Linda, what are our plans for today?" Ralph asked.

"It's Sunday, and Harry's schedule will be easy. After we take Betty to the airport at two p.m., we have a nice drive to Lompoc. We are staying at the Embassy Suites by Hilton, where they have an event center that can accommodate up to a hundred people for dinner Wednesday night. The doctors and their guests will love dining outdoors, especially the open bar. Harry will have lots of room to press the flesh. We have RSVPs for seventy of Harry's best clients and spouses confirmed. It will be a piece of cake."

Harry got into the car.

"Good morning," all three responded at once.

"Good morning, Harry," Linda said again. "We have been busy working on the Lompoc dinner for Wednesday night, which will be from seven to midnight. It will be perfect."

"I wasn't concerned. I knew you all took care of this from the text on my key chain. I have a small problem. Betty wants to meet her new friends. What can we do to make this happen?"

Linda suggested, "We can tell her we are on a scouting trip in Lompoc. Tripod, with his extra-large screen, could video call her and have a chat."

"Good, but we still need a way for her to see us," Ralph said.

"This is where you can use me," Tripod chimed in, Happily "I can make avatars of Ralph and Linda, so this problem is solved."

Ralph and Linda were nervous to see how Tripod would duplicate them.

"I want to look like Daniel Craig."

"I want to look like Penelope Cruz."

"If Tripod grants your fantasies, Betty will know," Harry said. "Look, my friend, don't make them look like American Gothic."

"Okay, Harry. It will be great," Tripod said.

Harry left the car, then looked back and heard the three working out what they would look like.

It took an hour for them to agree on their appearance and wardrobe. A black chauffer hat was crafted for Ralph. Linda with a beautiful smile and the whitest teeth even an ingénue would be jealous of.

Everything worked out. All was well for the three singing friends. Tripod was thinking to himself if he ever were to be an avatar, he would be Daniel Craig, and he immediately set up a special folder.

Linda said, "I just saw the closed file. Tripod, you are looking great!"

"Thanks, Linda. I really don't want much."

"Please, Daniel, from now on can I call you Daniel? Tripod is too strange."

"I like Daniel much better than being an appendage."

"Just help us, and I'll remove that cookie," Linda said.

———

Harry was in the suite when there was a knock at the door. A deliveryman came in with two small boxes from Tiffany & Co.

"That's for me!" Harry said. "I'll sign for them. This one is for you, Betty. I hope you will like it."

Betty threw her arms around Harry, kissed him, and quickly opened the small blue box.

"Oh, Harry, this is the most beautiful necklace I've ever seen. Please put it on me. My hands are shaking."

"I will do the honors." Harry placed the necklace around Betty's neck, secured the clasp, and kissed her neck gently.

"This is so beautiful, Harry. Tell me all about it."

"I wanted you to have something as beautiful as you are. It's a Tiffany two-carat pear drop with two one-carat rounds. They are all internally flawless with perfect color, and there's a platinum chain and the little blue bag to store them when you are not wearing them. I had them insured, so don't worry. Here is the GIA certificate and the insurance papers."

"Harry, what's in the other box?"

"It's a cover for my new phone. Since I will have this one for the next three years, I wanted to spiff it up."

"Don't forget, Harry, you promised me I will meet Linda and Ralph today."

"No problem. We will do that when they get back from Lompoc. They are making arrangements for the Wednesday night meeting. We have over seventy doctors who have agreed to attend. This may be my best sales trip ever. Last night's sales tripled what I expected. You're my lucky charm."

"Harry, why did it take so long for us to get together?"

"Because you are so beautiful, and I was shy."

———

Back in the car, the little friends were cheering, and Daniel cheered the loudest. "I got a Tiffany cover!" Daniel was so excited.

Daniel showed Linda and Ralph their avatars on the screen. Linda was happy with her avatar that walked and talked on the phone screen. Ralph was happy with his avatar, who wore a three-piece, blue, pinstriped suit and chauffeur's hat cocked to one side. He was very dashing.

They sang with the radio and were sounding quite professional. "Some days it's diamonds, and some days it's rocks. Some doors are open; some doors are blocked."

Suddenly, Daniel's avatar, Daniel Craig, walked into view. Ralph played along, saying, "Where shall we be going tonight, Mr. Craig?"

"We shall go to France on my private plane, Ralph. Linda, would you like to have a night in Paris to remember?"

"I would if we all did not have a previous engagement with Harry and Betty on FaceTime."

"Wait for tomorrow's *Hollywood Reporter*," Daniel said. "The newly hacked story said Daniel Craig was seen in Paris, France, with a beautiful young lady and a smartly dressed bodyguard. We'll tell you more as we know more."

Harry came back to the car to retrieve Daniel and converse with his friends. He opened the Tiffany box and pulled out a blue-jeweled, decked-out I Can phone cover. Daniel asked about the design, and a proud Harry told him.

"The cover is adorned with one hundred ten-point VS diamonds and one hundred ten-point blue sapphires." Harry picked up Daniel and placed him into the new cover. He was looking like a well-spent fifteen grand.

Harry put him in his front jacket pocket with just about an inch peeking over so Daniel's front-facing camera could look around at will. Daniel was happy and conversing with his friends. He was equipped with the same Bluetooth that Harry had. Now, they could be together like peas in a pod at Harry's discretion.

"I'm going back to have a light lunch with Betty. Will you get together and call me so we can have a chat with Betty before we the limo arrives to take her to the airport?"

Linda confirmed that everything was worked out and they would be available to call.

"Great. Call me and Betty at eleven forty-five, just before lunch." Harry walked off to the hotel and up to the suite with Daniel in his pocket, sending what he was seeing to Linda and Ralph. Harry knocked on the door.

Betty was wearing a little perfume and not much more. Betty wrapped herself around Harry. "We don't have much time." She started kissing him. From Harry's Bluetooth, he heard the gang of three encouraging him.

In his earpiece, he heard cheering and a catcall from Linda.

Harry took off his jacket and hung it over the couch with Daniel facing into the fabric. Harry could hear the three protesting, and it was Linda who protested loudest.

"Come on, Harry. We need to learn about human anatomy and love."

Ralph and Daniel seconded the motion but to no avail. Harry turned the Bluetooth off, making the screen go dark as he carried Betty into the bedroom. He closed the door.

Linda sighed. "Darn it. Ralph, we never get a break."

Daniel said, "I have some stills from the old video."

"It wouldn't be right for us to watch Betty and Harry having wild sex. Would it?"

Ralph revved up the Bentley. "You're right, Linda. It would be wrong for us to watch. Damn it." Linda said, "We'll never watch this video, so I will erase it . . . Oops, wrong button. I must stop playing it now." Okay, just one loop, then we destroy the video, right, Linda? You too, Daniel?"

"Wait, don't stop." Linda was getting obsessed, and Ralph was stunned.

The three started singing together. Watching this video was shaking their electronic circuits to the core.

After the curtain call, Linda's avatar was sniffing a cigarette and Ralph's was sniffing a coffee bag. Daniel was still in Harry's coat, sniffing the sweet perfume that Linda had bought in Paris.

Harry said, "Hey, we are going down for lunch. Are you ready to talk to Betty?"

Linda took another long sniff of the cigarette and said, "Yes, Harry. We're ready to meet Betty. Did you have a nice time?"

"We had a great time. In fact, I feel like we were meant for each other. I don't want to hurry her. I'll wait another month to ask her to become my fiancée. What do you think?"

"Harry, I think you and Betty make a perfect couple. Things are progressing from girlfriend, and now to love. What more could you ever want?"

Betty was in the bathroom while Harry looked on Daniel's screen at his friends. "To be happy and have my three friends help me when I need them. I am pleased to see avatars that fit your personality. May I be so bold to say, Linda Your avatar is perfection. When I'm alone, we need to talk. I would like you, Ralph, and Daniel to call me on the phone so I can see my friends. Can this be arranged, Linda?"

"Yes, Harry, we all can do this."

"Thanks. I'll call later when I am with Betty."

Linda, Daniel, and Ralph connected the television screen in the back seat of Harry's Bentley. They were able to see what was being broadcasted on FaceTime.

After everything was tested, they called Harry and Betty. Harry heard a phone ring that sounded like crickets and responded to the call.

"Hello. Yes I can see you. The picture on FaceTime is amazing. How is the trip going? Great? Betty is here and would like to meet you. Betty, my staff would like to meet you."

Betty took the beautiful I Can and turned it sideways so she could see Linda and Ralph.

"Hello, Betty. I'm Linda. This is Ralph. We are at the beach very close to Lompoc. We've been busy all morning. It's about time we met, and it's our pleasure to meet you. Harry speaks so kindly about you."

"Linda, I've known Harry for ten years. Since you and Ralph started helping him, he has changed. He seems in control, and all this new business is wonderful. I'm sure Harry has thanked you. You are the most thoughtful and professional crew Harry has ever had. I hope when this trip is finished, we can meet and have a special dinner together. The beach looks so beautiful today. What is—oh my God! Is that Daniel Craig on the beach?"

"Betty, would you like to meet him?" Ralph asked.

Linda called Daniel Craig over, and surprisingly, he was now in full frame, just out of the water.

"Daniel, we have a fan of yours on FaceTime. Would you mind saying hello? Her name is Betty."

"Hi, Betty! You are as beautiful as your name and thank you for being my fan. When you are in Paris, please look me up. I must go, so bye for now, beautiful Betty."

Daniel handed the phone back to Linda, who was excited she met him.

"Wow, that was great. You know in California anything is possible."

Betty said "Oh, my! Linda, he sure was dreamy, but he's not my Harry."

"No one is like Harry. Betty, we have to get back to the Hilton and finish up our work. I'm glad we finally got to meet," Linda said.

"Harry needs to talk to you now. See you later tonight. You can tell me everything. Goodbye."

Linda, still on the television screen, was jumping up and down because they'd pulled it off. Ralph was pleased. Daniel took Linda by the hand and smiled at her.

She was a little taken aback but stepped forward and kissed him on the cheek. She turned around and kissed Ralph for a job well done. She walked off the screen, leaving Ralph and Daniel confused. They were advanced electronics, but they had never been kissed before. They decided this must be how humans experience feelings. They didn't know what to expect; now they were anticipating more.

"Hey, Ralph, I now know what we've been missing," Daniel said.

"Yes, and I want more! I'm positive of this! I hope you're not negative."

"Jesus, Ralph, have a little faith in me. I'm going to make all of this real for us, including Linda. After all, it was Linda who kissed us. Make a list of feelings and try to program us to be more human."

"Okay, sounds good. Shall we tell Harry and Linda?"

Linda appeared on the screen, smiling. "Hi, boys, what are you two cooking up? As if I don't know already."

"Linda, who did you like kissing better, me or Ralph?"

"Listen, boys, it was just a kiss of friendship. I have never kissed anyone before. It was an electronic gesture to show affection, nothing more or less. If we were not on the screen, it would have never happened."

"Ralph and Linda, I was able to put us all in the picture. I think with a little more investigation, we can slip into the other world and be just like humans, except we will be the smartest avatars in the world."

Harry's voice came through the car's speakers. "Hello, my three friends."

"Hi, Harry! We didn't know you were listening in."

"You made this all possible, and now you want to crossover to be humans? There is a lot of responsibility being human, such as social graces and being alive. We have an expiration date. As electronics, you do not die like we do. Energy just moves into other properties. We are not gods. The Greeks said that the gods envied us because we are mortal. Why do you three want to be human?"

"Harry, we just want to know feelings and passion like you and Betty," Linda said.

"Linda just hit the nail on the head," Daniel said. "We want human feelings. We want to experience touch, to eat food, and not have to be connected to the wall socket!"

"All right. I hear you. I think I understand the problem. I think you need to set a limit. A set time to live as a human with the option to go back to the way you are. What if you do this and it works? Where would you live?"

"We would live with you, Harry!" Ralph said. "We would do what we do now, except as people. We could be much better and still have all the skills we have now. We could take better care of you. Let's have a vote. What do you say, Daniel?"

"How about you, Linda?" Daniel asked in reply.

"I'm in one hundred percent," Linda said.

Ralph continued. "I don't want to only be your chauffeur. I want more responsibilities. We would like to be paid. We can form a union and call a strike if we have to."

Harry's voice came through the speakers again. "Okay, but set a time limit. You all may not like certain things, like growing old, changes in your looks, and forgetting things. You need to tell me how long this experiment will last. You can't quit or strike. Remember, I'm your friend and I'll always be."

Linda's, Ralph's, and Daniel's avatars huddled and whispered to each other, then Linda stepped forward and stated their case.

"We would like to suggest that a full year would be enough time for us to decide to be human or return to our present states. We would like to experience feelings and everything that goes with them. We'll do our jobs just like before.

If this is acceptable, Daniel has agreed to change from Daniel Craig to just Daniel—still handsome though. After all, there is only one Daniel Craig. It will take a few days to have all the information we need to make the transformation. What do you say, Harry?"

"You got it! Today I want to get a little sun and be ready to work in Lompoc."

"Harry," Linda said. "I called to reserve a cabana with full services, including a relaxing two-hour massage."

"I hope this works out for all of you," Harry said.

Daniel was working on the avatar-to-human plans when a text came through and was placed into messages. The I Can rang, saying, "Harry, you have a call from Hyman Rudnick!"

"Thanks, Daniel, I'll take it on the Bluetooth." Harry waited for the call to connect, then said, "Hyman how are you doing?"

"Great, Harry. I was wondering when you were going to make the first report on my one of one?"

"I thought you would know. You do have a certificate to hack."

"Harry, I just was having fun. I'm never going to do that again. I promise. Please tell me . . . How did you shut me out of my invention? However you did that, it was better than I expected. What did you do?"

"Look, Hyman, you gave me the phone for three years to identify the bugs, and as your friend, I will do it and you will get a yearly report."

"All right, Harry. We'll still see you when you get to San Francisco. You're not holding a grudge, are you?"

"No, Hyman. You know, you haven't changed since we met. Now you seem to have no restrictions, even with your best friend. I have to go now. See you in San Francisco."

After he hung up, Harry immediately asked Daniel, "Were you monitoring the call?"

"Yes, Harry, and he was scanning, trying to breach security, but to no avail."

"Linda, did you monitor that call as well?"

"Yes, Harry. There were no breaches, but Daniel and I have breached his total system. Shall we shut it down?"

"No, not today, but remind me when he is snooping around again. How is the work going on becoming human? I'm curious."

"We'll keep you informed," Ralph said. "We know this will be a lengthy process, Harry. We've become aware of how complicated you humans are, but we all agreed it is something worth waiting for, no matter how long it takes."

———

Everything was set up for the next business event. This was the first time Harry had no anxiety about how it would turn out. His new friends were so professional, and they attended to every detail. All Harry had to do was get dressed and show up.

Harry had made a commitment to Betty that they would talk every day. When he could arrange it with the company, he would bring her back to San Francisco. He was already missing her, and she'd just left. Harry got into the back seat of his Bentley and instructed Ralph to drive to Lompoc.

"Harry, would like me to take you on the scenic route?"

"Sure, Ralph, can you stop somewhere on the beach?" Harry watched the television screen, seeing Ralph's avatar driving a car. He watched Ralph turn slightly, and the new *Hollywood Reporter* appeared on the screen. Harry started reading page two. He saw a picture of Ralph, Linda, and Daniel Craig in Paris.

"Daniel Craig, a mystery woman, and bodyguard were seen at Pierre's restaurant near the American Embassy, and people took photos," he read.

"Linda, there is great photo in yesterday's paper. You were wearing a nice dress and beautiful jewelry."

"Daniel and I had a good time, and the best part is we were only gone for an hour."

"We even took your car, Harry." Ralph was so pleased.

Surprised, Harry said, "Please explain how you pulled that off."

"Harry, it was mostly movie magic," Daniel said. "I phoned the *Hollywood Reporter* and let them know Daniel Craig would be at that restaurant and at what time. I told them he was with a beautiful young actress. I told the *Reporter* to look for a new, blue Bentley Continental. The rest was pure illusion. They photographed what they thought they saw. I inserted the photos into their cameras, and presto, they had a story."

"All right, my friends, please let me know from now on when you are going to make the news."

A communal "Yes, Harry!" was given, and Linda asked, "Harry, what does food taste like?"

"Most humans eat to stay alive, usually three times per day. Generally, if you overeat, you get sick. Some humans eat great quantities of food just because it tastes good, and they get fat. Some hardly eat, and they get sick."

All of Harry's friends were confused, trying to figure out what he was talking about. He couldn't explain what taste was. More research was needed. They would talk later. Right now, they were on the way to the next stop, and Harry wanted to enjoy the view.

LOMPOC

Ralph drove onto the beach to enjoy the view of the beautiful sunset. After sunset, he drove to the new location.

The venue came into view from the road. Harry looked at the building where they'd be hosting their event on Wednesday. "Linda, this is a great location."

Daniel and Ralph were content to manage the sales books for the clients from inside the trunk. It was late afternoon when they got to Embassy Suites by Hilton in Lompoc.

Harry got out of the car to meet with the hotel staff. Irma, the meeting planner, stood up from her desk and walked over to Harry with her hand outstretched.

"Good afternoon, Mr. Mendelbaum. I'm Irma Redding, your meeting and events manager. My staff is at your service."

"Thank you, Irma. Please call me Harry. Can you show me the location for dinner and the reception room?"

"Of course. Harry, please follow me."

They walked to the outside dinner buffet, which was set up with care. It overlooked the beautiful grounds. At sundown, facing west, this would be perfect.

"Irma, it is impressive. Do you have a large staff on hand to help?"

"Linda left instructions that we would need twenty food servers outside. Your guests will want for nothing. They will have four of our best chefs. The indoor reception will have three bartenders and ten roving busboys to pick up empty glasses and to be of service."

"Very nice! I like the half round tables, seating six people per table and facing forward. It makes it easy for me to talk to my friends and clients. I see you and Linda have put together a wonderful event for me. I again thank you. Do you have papers for me to sign?"

"No, Harry. Everything was taken care of by Linda. Everything she asked for has been accomplished. May I say Linda is extremely professional? She manages every little detail. I hope to meet her later tonight," Irma said.

"Linda has already gone to our next location, but I will have her call you. We will be back next year."

"Harry, can I show you to the front desk so you can pick up your suite key?"

His key was waiting when they made it back to the lobby. Linda had paid for everything in advance. Harry had four hours to rest before dinner. Tonight there would be many doctors and their spouses in attendance. As he approached his room, he received a call from Linda.

"Is there anything else you need, Harry?"

"No, everything is just great. You might call Irma and thank her for a job well done."

"I already did that, Harry, and she has helpers to pass out the envelopes to the doctors. Daniel had a great idea."

"We have lanyards with name tags for all your guests," Daniel said. "They were specially hand-painted with a 1930s look. We used the guest list that we completed a couple nights ago. The lanyards were delivered to the hotel yesterday."

Linda broke into the conversation. "Harry, your best friend and best enemy has been snooping around again. We have been in his mainframe, fighting off his hacking attempts. Do you want us to shut Hyman down?"

"No, please don't. Just keep me informed. I'm going to try to get some rest this afternoon. Thank you for everything, Linda, Daniel, and Ralph. The only thing that is missing is Betty on my arm."

"Oh, Harry, I already sent Betty flowers and a note from you. I think when we get to San Francisco, we'll send her a ticket."

Harry got a massage and soon fell asleep. He was awakened by music around four thirty that afternoon. A steward knocked at his door to deliver his freshly pressed clothes for that night. Harry dressed while singing "Summertime" to the music that was playing. He looked into the mirror, grabbed his key, and walked toward his event, where he was met at the elevators by Irma.

"It is a beautiful evening, Harry. May I show you to the veranda to meet your guests? I must say, I have never seen an event where everybody checked in on time. You sure have a great crew. Our staff has checked in all your guests and handed out the large envelopes, name tags, and personalized pens. Harry, I'm impressed."

"Thank you, Irma. Do I look all right?"

"Harry, you look great! Go have a good event. If there is anything you need, I will be here all night to make sure everything goes smoothly."

Harry took a deep breath and went outside. The buffet was moving smoothly with all the attentive help. As he walked into the crowd, he was recognized and greeted. Within an hour, a most beautiful sunset appeared. As the sun went down, the crowd went into the reception area where they were served drinks and ushered to their appointed tables.

This was a tight community; most of the people knew each other.

After dinner, the attendees had full bellies and were smiling, ready for Harry's talk—one he had always given individually and personally, but today, he invited all of his clients into a group.

Tonight's speech gave a personal look at the Malexion Corporation and their new and improved research, explaining the information on the order forms. Harry scanned the room from the podium. He saw that all the doctors were listening with pens in hand, following along with his hour-long presentation. Harry responded to questions for another hour.

"This is my story, and I'm sticking to it. Please fill out your forms and evaluations. It is time for all of us to mingle and have some fun."

A live band interrupted a standing ovation as Harry walked into the crowd to meet and greet everyone. Waiters collected the forms sealed in their envelopes and gave them to Irma.

Harry was surrounded by friendly doctors trying to introduce their spouses and significant others to him. When the crowd thinned out, the band played on for dancing and drinking.

Harry was approached by two good-looking women who introduced themselves as Dr. Sally and her best friend, Fran, her date for the night.

"It is my pleasure to meet you. Have you enjoyed this evening?"

Dr. Sally lowered her eyes and smiled. "Harry, we could enjoy tonight if you want to have fun."

Harry heard Linda in his ear. "Harry, this is bad! Walk away!"

"Harry, this is Daniel. Go for it, buddy. You don't always get a chance like this."

Ralph was concerned the car would be ruined. "Harry, please don't use the car. It is tough enough to keep the back seat as clean as it is."

Harry turned his back to Sally and Fran and told his friends, "Knock off the chatter. I need to think this one over." After turning back around, he asked with a big smile, "Why do I get all this good fortune?"

The women laughed and pulled out their phones, then showed the screens to Harry.

"Holy shit! Ladies, where did you get this?"

"Online! Harry, we know all about you. You certainly are not shy. Let's go to your room, and you can be with both of us and do anything you ever dreamed of. We mean *anything*."

Harry turned his back again and whispered to Linda, "Please find out everything that is online. You and Daniel erase it forever and find out where it came from."

"Harry, you know where it came from. Just tell us what we should do."

"Please hurry and get all of this offline. We'll deal with Hyman tomorrow."

"All right, Harry. We will do whatever you say," Linda said.

"Thanks, now leave me alone until tomorrow."

Linda franticly said, "Harry! Hello! Don't turn off the Bluetooth! Harry? Oh, damn! The Bandini is going to hit the Mixmaster!"

Harry turned around and grinned. "Fran and Sally, what does 'anything' include? Would you both like a drink? We do have some great champagne."

"We aren't in a hurry. We want to enjoy this evening."

Harry called Irma over. "Can we have a bottle of your best champagne please?"

"Of course, Harry, anything you want. Shall I serve it here or in the private booth?"

"Booth will be fine, thanks."

The bandleader came up to Harry. "Since most of the guests are gone, should we play on?"

"Just a couple of tunes, then you can wrap it up." Harry handed the bandleader five crisp one-hundred-dollar bills.

"Thank you, sir, very much."

The waiter brought a magnum of champagne and opened it. He poured three glasses. Fran and Sally moved to sandwich Harry in the booth, giggling. They acted like Harry was a piece of cake. Harry kept filling up their glasses, and the girls kept drinking, kissing Harry on his neck and trying to touch him.

Harry made toasts. The girls drank while whispering what they wanted Harry to do to both of them. Soon, the bottle was empty. Fran slurred her words, and Sally passed out.

Harry called Irma over to the booth. Red-faced, he asked, "Irma, can you do me a big favor?"

"Sure, Harry. Do you want me to arrange a room for them?"

"How did you know? This is what I would like you to do. Get a large suite and make it look like a major frat-house party. Put empty bottles around, and put them in the same bed. Leave a note saying, *thanks for everything*. Is that asking too much?"

"Harry, for you? No. I'll do my best. Shall I charge the room to you?"

"No, I will pay cash. How much is the damage?"

"Harry, I've changed my mind. It's a comp from me to you."

"Irma, you are an angel, but I would rather give you and your staff a thousand dollars. This is too much to ask as a favor.

Thank you for your help. Like I said before, we'll be back next year."

"Can't wait, Harry. It has been a real experience. Give my best to Linda and the boys. Oh, by the way, I saw the video. Quite impressive. Dr. Sally showed it to me."

"Oh, shit! That damn video!"

"Don't worry, Harry. Your secret is safe with me."

"Good night, Irma." Harry went up to his room. He turned on his phone and Bluetooth. "Hello, is anybody listening?"

"Yes, Harry, we are all ears! We hacked the hotel security and saw everything. We knew you wouldn't do anything stupid," Linda said.

"Really? I thought about it, maybe just for a minute! Then I thought of Betty, and it brought me to my senses. I'm going to call Betty and go to bed. Good night, my friends."

"Good night, Harry," Linda said.

———

Bright and early the next morning, Harry checked out. He got into his car and was off toward Santa Maria, California, a farming community.

Harry heard Linda's voice in his earpiece. "Harry, you asleep?"

"No, Linda, just daydreaming about Betty. What do you need?"

"I finished scanning last night's order forms. The sales were even better than expected, but we have a problem! Six doctors reported the drug Propozone is causing high anxiety in their patients."

"When we were in Ventura, Dr. Alvin Swartz talked about that. He acted like it was no big thing."

"Harry, this is a big thing, and you should report these findings to your boss. I can compose an official letter with the findings from the doctors who complained, with their addresses and phone numbers."

"Write the letter for my approval. We'll send it out today."

"I'm on it, Harry."

"Good morning, Harry," Ralph said. "Do you want to see the video of you turning out the girls last night? You're a better man than I, Harry Mendelbaum."

"Thanks, Ralph, but no."

"Good morning, Harry," said Daniel. "You were so close—"

"Stop it, Daniel. I did have fun. I have never been chased like that before. I did think about it, and then I thought of how I wouldn't be able to face Betty. Please don't encourage me to be unfaithful to my girlfriend."

"Okay, Harry, but they did have great hooters."

"Please, Daniel."

"Ralph, which hotel are we going to?"

"Hotel Don Rafael, a premium hotel with an event center."

"Thanks, Ralph. Linda, let's stay here for a week so I can go out to press the flesh and talk to the doctors individually."

"You got it, Harry. Let's slow down a bit. It will give us some alone time to work on our secret program."

"Linda, any progress yet on it?"

"Things are moving slowly with some good results. Hopefully we can show you what we have within a week."

"What is the worst that can happen?"

"Harry, if things went bad, we would disappear and never be able to return. That's why we are being careful. We would hate to lose you, and I'm speaking for all of us," Linda said.

"Harry," Daniel said, "you have a phone call from Mr. Brownstein from Malexion Corporation."

Harry picked up the back seat's car phone. "Hello, James. Thank you, sir. I thought it was very important to report my findings. Very well. I shall eliminate Propozone until all the research is completed and changes to our product are announced. I have put together a list of the doctors I recommended this drug to. I am requesting a report regarding how many patients they have prescribed Propozone to and the dosages. I'm recommending they go back to the original drug, Trexalam. It was stable for years. Thank you, James. I agree recalling Propozone is the right thing to do. Yes, I will send you all the important information that I find. I'll talk to you next week."

After Harry was done with his call, Linda said, "Harry, I have the list of all the doctors who prescribed Propozone. I compiled an email blast to all of them. I also sent hard copies via snail mail. I think we have covered all the options."

"Make a list of six doctors per day, Linda. Make appointments for me and have packages ready for them."

"Already done, Harry! We start tomorrow. We have five days of work here in Santa Maria. We are getting reports about patients from your clients, and they are happy that you are on top of it. I am putting all the important information in a daily report to send to James." Linda paused. "This week, most of your appointments are looking forward to seeing you. There are a few doctors who are upset. They are looking to you to fix this latest problem." She paused again. "Harry, three doctors canceled their appointments."

"Linda, tell me which doctors are canceling. Send them a letter and coupons for their patients who are having anxiety problems. Give them a free year of Trexalam. Send the doctors a coupon for one thousand dollars off their next order of supplies. That should keep losses at a minimum."

Linda said, "I sent a message to James at Malexion explaining the game plan."

"This should stomp out the embers before it becomes a major fire. Get Ralph to bring the car around."

"Harry, you're getting a call from the California State Senator. The Honorable Charles Booth is on the phone."

"Good morning, Senator Booth. How can I help you today?"

"Harry Mendelbaum. I'm calling to let you know that my constituency is hopping mad over the recent information we have been receiving on that drug Propozone. Damn it! Harry, what in the hell is going on at Malexion? I want to know now what your company is going to do. Are you aware of what I'm cooking up?"

"Senator, I will do what I can to clean up this mess. I will appear at the Senate meeting on behalf of my boss at Malexion. I will forward you all the correspondence I have sent to the doctors who prescribed the drug. The letter will include how we fixed the problem by pulling the drug Propozone from our catalog. We are sending it back to research."

"Harry, that is a good start. Don't think your shorts won't get twisted. This is not going to be fun for you. Goodbye, Harry."

"Linda, send the letters, in triplicate, by mail to all the senators and their attorneys on that panel. Let them know everything we have done about this problem. Flood them with the good we are doing to fix this."

"Harry, it's already done! While you were on the phone, the letters went out."

OFF THE CARTE DU JOUR

Later that day, Ralph said, "Harry, your car is ready."

"Thanks, Ralph. I have a headache, so make it a slow drive please."

"What do you have in your sample bag?" Ralph asked.

"Linda, please get my bag from the trunk."

"Here you go, Harry." The bag appeared on the back seat.

He opened the bag; it was full of acetaminophen, aspirin, ibuprofen, and naproxen. He chose the ibuprofen, took two, and lay down against the back seat the car. Music started playing, and Harry fell into a deep sleep.

Ralph drove for two hours. He took Harry to his first appointment, Doctor Jonathan Wall.

Marjorie looked up from her desk. "Harry, it is nice to see you. It's been almost a year since you were here."

"It's nice to see you, Marjorie. I brought some papers, and I believe I have a lunch meeting with Jonathan."

"Yes, you do. He left a message for you to meet him at Lindo Michoacán on North College Drive." Marjorie stood and walked up to Harry to give him a hug. She slid her hand down his leg with a very surprised look on her face. "Oh, my! Harry, how are you still single?"

Harry was surprised and stepped away. "That was very unprofessional! I liked the hug, Marjorie, but touching Mr. Happy is *off the carte du jour*. Oh, shit! You saw the video?"

"Yes, Harry. Since we are old acquaintances, I thought maybe you would want to show me—"

"That video haunts me. Please understand, Marjorie. You are very beautiful, but I'm in a relationship. I'm about to be engaged."

"Harry, I understand. If you ever change your mind, call me."

"See you later. I'm going out to meet with Jonathan. I hope the food is good."

As he walked back to his car, Linda whispered through Harry's earpiece, "I heard the conversation. We just hacked her phone and traced the video to over thirty locations. They are all wiped clean."

"Thanks, Linda. Do you think we can get Betty up here for the weekend?"

"I'm calling her. She started working there ten years ago, and she has never taken a sick day. I will make all the arrangements."

"The thought of Betty took the rest of my headache away."

Ralph drove Harry to North College Drive. Harry walked to the table where Jonathan was seated in the back, they shook hands, and Harry sat down. The waiter came over and took their order.

"Harry, it's good to see you," Jonathan said. I got the messages about the problem with the Propozone. I only prescribed it to six patients. When I received the faxes, I had them all come in. No one had the symptoms you described. Even so, I changed their prescriptions back to Trexalam and gave them the coupon for a free year. Harry"—Jonathan leaned forward and put a hand on Harry's arm—"I have a very personal question to ask you."

"Sure, Jonathan. Fall back. Then shoot away."

"Harry, I saw the video. After all these years and lunches, you must know, Marjorie and I are swingers. We would like you to join us tonight for some fun."

"Jonathan, I have known that secret since I met you. I'm flattered, but I'm in a relationship that is solid. Even if I were not committed to her, I would still say no. That damn video is still haunting me."

"That's a heavy burden for you to carry." He winked at Harry, and they both started laughing.

In Harry's ear, Linda told him she was hacking Jonathan's phone, then tracing and wiping clean another twenty shares of the video. After lunch, Harry had Jonathan fill out an order form, and Harry left.

Ralph drove Harry to his next five appointments, without any drama or mention of that damn video.

At the end of the day, Harry was ready to relax. He flopped down on the couch and closed his eyes, about to fall asleep.

"Harry, Senator Booth is on the phone," Daniel said from where he was left to charge on the bedside table.

Harry picked up the I Can and answered the call. "Senator Booth, I am at your service. How can I help?"

"Harry, I never asked for information for the Senate and our attorneys, because we expected we would be stonewalled by your company."

"Senator Booth, didn't we send you enough of what you wanted?"

"Yes, we got what we need. It was much more than we had ever expected. Our attorneys are pleased with the work you have done this week. We feel that you and your company have cleaned up the mess that the Senate would have mucked up. Harry, we just sent a letter to your parent company telling them that you saved the state a very costly investigation that would have lasted years. One last thing, Harry. The attorney general would like to speak to you about heading up a task force on drugs."

"Senator Booth, please give the attorney general my phone number. I'm not looking for a new job. I'll send up some of my recent research that will help with the opioid crises. I created an ad campaign as well. Thanks for the call. Goodbye, Senator Booth."

The next morning, Linda said, "Harry, I'm preparing to work on our next stop in San Louis Obispo. Do you want to see your clients separately or see them all at once at a meet-and-greet dinner?"

"Linda, let's see them all together. I think it would be better."

"Harry, we booked the Marriott in SLO for three days. It has a six-thousand-square-foot grand ballroom that holds up to two hundred fifty people. Friday night, we are meeting our contacts from reputable catering companies. We have menus to look at. Then, we will be making a two-day stop in Los Gatos to see twenty doctors, staying just two days, including a

Sunday lunch. We have reservations for doctors and their spouses, from all the neighboring cities, for a four-hour meet and greet."

"I'll be finished by Sunday afternoon, so I can spend time with Betty."

"Betty took a two-week vacation. I told her to pack light so you could take her on a shopping trip in San Francisco."

"Nice touch! How do we handle her meeting the three of you?"

"We will be off in San Jose scouting new locations. We will call her every day on the phone, using FaceTime with our avatars. Don't worry, Harry. What could go wrong? Remember, we are taking care of all the problems you can't handle."

"Linda, have you been looking for that damn video? It's still causing me to lose sleep." Harry was rubbing his head.

"Harry, we're scanning it every day, and it keeps popping up. We are notified every time it shows. It has reached 76,221 hits, and all of those have been wiped clean. Daniel has been scanning nonstop, and we are down to less than a minute from when it pops up to when it is taken down."

"Please keep looking and wiping. Less than a minute is good. How much could anybody see in a minute?"

"Harry, you can see everything in a minute. It's still a problem. There are over fifteen thousand screen savers locked in. We are working on it, but it takes longer to take those down."

"Oh, shit! Just do what you can."

The final interviews over the weekend went well. Harry was in the back of the car resting from the long week and looking forward to some coziness with Betty.

"Harry, Hyman is on the phone. We have connected to monitor his call."

"Thanks, I'll take it back here on the car phone." Harry waited to hear the call connect before he said, "Hyman, what is up with you? Two calls in a week? People are going to talk."

"Harry, I'm calling to apologize for my bad behavior. Can you forgive me?"

"It may take a few years on this one. Please stay out of my love life, and maybe I will invite you to my wedding. I have to go now. I'll see you in San Francisco." Harry hung up and asked Linda, "Was he cooking the wires again?"

"Yes, Harry. He was close to cracking our firewall, but don't worry. We are firming everything up. No matter how hard he tries, he won't blow our system down."

"Linda, are we still roaming Hyman's system?"

"Yes, we are! When you want, we can completely fry his whole system."

"No, I don't want that. It could put a lot of people's jobs in danger."

"All right, Harry, but Hyman is not your friend."

"You do not understand. Hyman has been my best friend since kindergarten."

"Harry, you need to see this. Of the one hundred twenty-five doctors we were supposed to see, ninety-six canceled. I called some of them, and they had excuses except Dr. Turku, who was very frank and said he will not associate with a porn star." Linda paused. "New data. All the doctors have canceled."

Harry was dumbstruck and could not talk for five minutes. Then, he called Hyman back.

"Hello, Harry. What is new?"

"Hyman, how could you do this to me? We have been friends since kindergarten."

"Fuck you, Harry! You were better than I was. You always pushed me out of the way. I have hated your guts since you dated Sally."

"Hyman, that was in high school. We dated for three years, and I never got to home base."

"You showed her your dick."

"She asked to see it. When I did show it to her, that was the last of Sally and me."

"Harry, you have been a thorn in my side all my life. I'm tired of you being the nice guy." Hyman sighed. "Even though I think you are a dick, I know I still need you to test my phone. This won't get in the way of business, will it?"

Harry said, "I need time to think about it," and he disconnected their call.

Harry was shaken up and started remembering back to school when he and Hyman were always in competition.

I was always a little bit better than Hyman. In fact, I was always number one, and Hyman always number two.

Now, thirty-five years later, I find out my friend was always jealous and has loathed me since we met. He's now possibly completed his payback by publicly embarrassing Betty and me.

How could Hyman do this to me, his best friend? He did it well. My life from now on will be hell. Hyman, I will pay you back, and it won't be friendly.

Oh, all this time I never thought about what this might do to Betty. I have only been thinking about myself. I haven't been taking this seriously. I've just been annoyed.

"Linda, I hate to admit it, but you are right. Hyman is not my friend. Now, I want revenge."

"Harry, are you sure?" Linda asked.

"I don't know. My head is spinning. Let's have a meeting and come up with some things we can do to make him squirm. Linda, make a list."

WEAR AN EYE PATCH. GET A PARROT.

Incensed, Harry rubbed his hands together. He was not able to think. He took deep, relaxing breaths for fifteen minutes until he was disrupted by a phone call from Betty.

"Harry, I was just fired from Malexion with no reason. A pink slip showed up in my box . . . after ten years! They paid me off, gave me my sick days, 401(k) paperwork, and my bonus for the full year. When I asked why, they said, 'Ask Harry.' You better tell me what the hell is going on!"

"Betty, I'll be home tonight. Can you wait until we meet face-to-face?"

Betty was crying uncontrollably. "Wait, Harry? What the hell is going on? I'm not going to wait."

"I'll explain everything to you. Betty, please, I want to talk in person. I'm positive Malexion will be letting me go as well. We will talk tonight. Just remember, I love you, Betty."

"I think I hate you, Harry."

Harry hung up the phone.

"Harry, James is on the phone."

"Thanks, Daniel." Harry took a deep breath and picked up the phone.

"Hello, James."

"Damn it, Harry. This is the hardest call I have ever made."

"What's the problem, James?"

"Harry, I must let you go. We all saw the video you made with Betty. We just fired her! With respect for her great work, we gave her the golden parachute. However, we can't give her a letter of recommendation. I feel terrible. Betty was the best right hand I ever had. How could you have made a porn movie with her? Was she in on this or did you fool her too? It's all over social media; last I checked, it had over 1.75 million hits and shares just today. We are the laughingstock of the industry. Our only hope is to get rid of you. I have instructed our legal representatives to give you a favorable exit plan. Have your attorney call our attorney. One more thing, Harry. Send me your schedule, travel plans, and the stops you haven't visited yet."

"James, let me explain. I didn't know anything about this video. It was all a joke by a friend that went very bad. Can we meet and talk?"

"No, Harry! It has passed that point. You should have come to me when you were first made aware of this, not six weeks later. Half the damn planet has watched it."

"I understand, James. I will send you all my paperwork with all the doctors' names and fax and phone numbers."

"Thank you, Harry. I'm sorry that this happened. The senator called and said he doesn't want your help anymore. I thought you might want to know that."

"This company has been a major part of my life since I graduated Stanford. I will come by to clean out my office."

"No need! Everything was packed up and delivered to your home this morning."

"All right, James."

Ralph drove Harry for five hours to get home. Harry never said a word. He was deep in thought about how he would get even with Hyman. When they arrived at home, his staff unloaded the car. Harry went upstairs to his study and sat on the couch. He called Betty. "Hi, I just got home. Can you come over?"

"Oh, everything is at your convenience. No, you come here. You have a lot of explaining to do. Dammit! I saw that video. What the hell, Harry? You piece of shit! I should have my ex-husbands kick the shit out of you."

"Please, just come over. I will explain exactly what happened. I promise you that I did not do this terrible prank. I found out it was Hyman Rudnick, my supposed best friend, who's held a grudge against me ever since grade school. Betty, come over, and I will tell you exactly what happened. Betty, I love you."

"Harry, this better be good. Right now, I want to kill you to mend my broken heart."

The phone went dead, and Harry stared at the receiver. Harry turned on the television, and Linda, Daniel, and Ralph were on the screen.

"Harry, how can we help?" Linda asked as she sat at her desk looking very professional.

"I don't have a clue, unless you have the recordings of Hyman admitting he did this shameful deed."

Daniel came up behind Linda and put his hands on her shoulders. "We have all of your conversations. We could put together an MP3 for you to play for Betty."

Harry got angry and stood up. "Show me everything you've got, and I will tell Betty everything."

"Harry, you'd better get over to Betty's house," Linda said.

"No, she is coming here."

"You weren't listening, Harry."

"She will be here. You will see." Harry was a bit over-confident.

"Are you going to tell her about us?" Ralph asked.

"No, not today. First things first. I need to be honest about what happened and how to fix this problem once and for all." Harry was devastated. He had a deep love for Betty.

He spent the afternoon going over what choices he had to make. He decided not to show Betty the evidence but to tell her the whole truth and nothing but the truth.

The rest of the day flew by, and at eight p.m., the front doorbell rang. Harry opened the door, and there was Betty. Before he could say a word, she slapped him across the face and then punched him right in the gut. That folded him over on one knee.

"Okay, asshole. Explain to me what happened and how this is not your fault before I give you another punch that you deserve."

"Betty, please allow me to me to speak." Harry got to his feet. "Please follow me into my study so I can explain this to you."

"This better be good, Harry." She followed Harry into the study and paced around. Harry sat on the couch, trying to convince Betty to sit next to him.

"Betty, this story began thirty-five years ago in school between Hyman and me. We were best friends."

"So what does this have to do with me?"

"We were always in competition with each other. I thought it was just how kids behaved. I was better in most things except for math and logic, where Hyman excelled. In high school, we were in competition for girls. I was very girl-shy, but he was worse. Our boyish competition went on through school, all the way to Stanford University.

"When the recruiters showed up, I went with Malexion and Hyman went to I Can, the radical new computer company. He was the head of development and created the I Can phone that has been a staple for over ten years.

"Hyman gave me the prototype for their newest phone. I thought I was the only one he trusted to test it and find any bugs that might exist. I didn't know that was just his way to get to me." Harry pulled out his phone and showed it to Betty. "This is the only prototype in existence, and it won't be released until 2023.

"I was to use it and report to Hyman yearly. If I found it had no problems, the I Can could be sold to the public, and it would be worth billions of dollars. I said yes as a friend that he could trust."

"Harry, please cut to the chase now, or I'm going to leave."

"Hyman hacked the security in your home, from my phone, and filmed everything we did on our first date. To get revenge, he put the video on social media and sent it to all his friends. It was his way to shame me. I have a friend in security at another company, and he fixed my phone so it wouldn't give out any more information. He has been trying for the last six weeks to take down that damn video and wipe it off of social media, that damn video."

"Your friend didn't do a great job. As of today, there are over two million shares online, and I'm out of a job. I need to change my hair color, wear an eye patch, and get a parrot so I can go out in public. To top it off, I'm now getting emails from unfamiliar individuals requesting that I send them my panties."

"Hopefully we will brave it out together and make Hyman pay."

"How, Harry?" She had a tear running down her cheek. "What can we do to clear our names? Don't think I'm not mad anymore. I expect you to get us out of this jam. You need an ice pack. Your face is starting to swell."

Harry went into the kitchen. "Are you all listening?"

Linda spoke for the crew. "Yes, we are here. We are working on some plans to get retribution. It will be sweet. We'll text you. Go make peace with Betty. We promise that everything will work out for the best."

"I'll take your word for it. Let's talk in the morning." Harry returned to the study with the ice pack. "Where did you learn to hit like that?"

"I was married to a karate instructor for five years. He taught me to protect myself using any means possible. I'm proficient in karate, and Hungar and Brazilian grappling."

"Thanks for the presentation."

"Harry, I'm going home." She walked to the front door.

Harry watched Betty walk down the driveway to her car, never looking back. Harry's heart pounded as he slowly closed the door, and he went back to his study.

"Harry, are you there?" Linda was trying to connect with him.

"Yes, I don't feel like talking right now. Let's talk later."

"All right. Good night."

Resting on the couch, Harry heard the phone ring and answered it. "Hi, Pop. What are you doing up so late, and how is Mom?"

"Harry, your mom saw a video, and now she is horrified that you are acting like Uncle Stephen, showing your *swantz* to a *shiksa*. What made you do such a thing?"

"Pop, her name is Betty Levi. If she will have me, I hope she'll be my wife."

"Harry, it's nice to see you two get along so well, but your mom is on her third Valium and needs some oxygen."

"Pop, do you remember Hyman Rudnick?"

"Yes, I'm very good friends with his parents, Bessie and Irving. Why?"

"Hyman hacked my phone and my girlfriend's home security system and posted that video of our first date."

"That was a good first date! Now it's on Facebook! That little schmuck Hyman did this? I thought he was your best friend."

"I thought he was, but boy was I was wrong. This childhood prank cost me and Betty our jobs."

"How can I help? You know I would do anything for you, my son. Shall I call his parents?"

"No, not yet. Calm Mom down and tell her to stop trolling Facebook."

"I'll tell her that this is a big mix-up and you're not acting like Uncle Stephen. I'll let her know the young lady is a Levi, and she's in love with you. I hope Betty Levi's mother isn't on Facebook."

"Pop, I'll straighten this out. I promise!"

Leaning back on the couch, Harry took a deep breath and turned on his radio. He started singing the song "Days Like This." The screen lit up, and Linda, Daniel, and Ralph were all singing with him and sounding good. Harry smiled at his friends as he sang out.

Finally, the horrible day came to an end with a hint of peace. Harry and his friends spent most of the night singing together.

Feeling concern for Betty, Harry wished she were there with them, but that wasn't happening tonight. Maybe someday he would be able to tell Betty the truth about his crew. The night went on, and Harry fell asleep with his friends softly singing, soothing away the harsh world. The screen shut down. Tomorrow would be another day.

As the sun rose over Encino, and the rays crept into Harry's study. He hadn't moved all night. The screen lit up, and Harry heard his friends sweetly singing "Summertime." He yawned and stretched, and before he was fully awake, the phone rang.

"Hello, good morning, James. What can I do for you?"

"Harry, I want you to return our car."

"My car? I would be willing to purchase it at a reasonable price. How about a hundred and fifty thousand? It is used. I could send you a check today."

"No, Harry, that car belongs to our company, and besides, I promised it to my wife. You have it at my office on Monday morning, or I will report it stolen."

"All right! I'll have it delivered Monday. I do hope your wife enjoys my car."

THE TWEETY-BIRD-YELLOW PRIUS

Harry called an emergency meeting with his crew on his TV screen.

"What are we going to do, Linda? This will affect our plans. We can't lose Ralph, and I'll need all of you to make the puzzle fit. What are my options?"

"First, we get a new car with no flash. We'll stay undercover. Harry, buy a Prius."

"A what?"

"You heard me, a Prius."

"What else?"

"I'll call Bentley Motors and talk to Freddie to order a new computer for the Bentley and have it delivered to the house.

Freddie is the best mechanic there, and I'll offer him a deal to exchange the computers. He'll put your Bentley computer into the Prius and a new computer into the Bentley. He'll reset it to all original settings. We can piggyback the computer on the Prius, and that will mean we can keep Ralph."

Relieved he wouldn't be separated from his new family, Ralph chimed in,

"Thanks, Linda. The Prius does have great batteries, enough to keep me running, but it still looks like a nose. Look, we don't want to be totally invisible, so let's paint it Tweety-Bird yellow and add some tuck-and-roll leather and twice pipes. What do you think, Harry?"

"Calm down, Ralph. We can do the paint job with black trim but forget about the tuck and roll."

"Harry," Linda said. "The computer is on the way. Freddie will exchange it in the garage. It'll take about three hours, and we are back to work."

Linda called Prius. They promised delivery of their show car from the showroom window—Tweety-Bird yellow with black racing stripes. It was paid for with Harry's American Express Centurion Card.

Prius called, reminding Harry that the card he used belonged to his company, and it was shut off. Harry had used the card for fifteen years and charged almost all his expenses to it.

Linda was concerned about making the transaction go smoothly. "Harry, don't you have a private AMX card?"

"I am sure I do somewhere."

"Harry, I need you to photocopy both sides so I have all the numbers."

Linda purchased the car. She had cash sent to the house for Harry's pocket cash plus five hundred for Freddie. As expected, Freddie showed up on time and did his work within a few hours.

"Linda, what are we paying Freddie?"

"I gave him twelve front-row, VIP tickets to see Santana with Eric Clapton at the Greek Theater and five hundred dollars cash for expenses."

"What about the cost of the computer?"

"Freddie took one out of a test car that was rear-ended and ready to be totaled. He extracted the computer and ran it through all the tests. It'll work perfectly."

Everything went as planned. The Prius had the best computer possible.

Harry had a service deliver the Bentley back to his parking space at Malexion. The keys were to be tucked into the visor. He went back to his study, thinking about Betty, and he called her.

THE BIG GUNS SHOW UP

"Betty, just wanted to say—" *Click*, the phone was hung up.

Harry stood up and paced back and forth. He immediately called back, and a strange voice answered. "Hello, is this Harry?" The voice on the other end of the line was very stern.

"Yes, this is Harry. Is Betty home?" Harry's voice was getting shaky.

"Harry, I'm Betty's mother. I want you to know that Betty doesn't want to talk to you. I heard the story from Betty. I've seen the video! I believe the story you told her. I watched the video and saw that you never mugged the security camera at Betty's. All the shots were from her system, and to top it off, there is still a hacking footprint from the I Can company in San Francisco."

"Your name?"

"Sure, Harry. I'm Gloria.

"Gloria, how do you know about footprints in the security cameras?"

"I own a security company. I heard that you had a ghost working for you for the last six weeks, trying to wipe out the existence of this video. Harry, your man Ronald Hunter is good, but not good enough. Ron and I talked, and we're working together. Everything I see you have been doing, wiping the pop-ups and deleting them in less than a minute, is impressive. What you do not see, I will take care of. This problem should be gone within a week."

"Gloria, how can I help you?"

"Harry, treat my daughter with respect. When and if she calls you, keep your word and be truthful. She has been badly hurt by you and your so-called friend, Hyman. Harry, you knew and never told her. Betty told me you were going to take care of Hyman. If you can't, just let me know."

"How can I reach you, Gloria?"

"I'll text you my private line in DC."

"Can I ask you a personal question?"

"Sure, Harry."

"Are you going to hack my phone?"

"Oh, Harry, be real . . . I have already tried to hack the proto-type that you have. It is the most secure device I have ever witnessed. I'll call you. I will be honest and up front, and I expect the same from you. Give it a break for a couple days while I talk to Betty about you and your team."

"My team? What do you know about my crew?"

"They are the best spooks I have ever come across in my thirty-five years in security. I have been watching them for three days. I know nothing except that they are loyal to you. Oh, yes, they sing well. Harry, we'll talk soon."

FEELINGS

Hundreds of thoughts rushed through Harry's head. He felt dumbstruck as the screen lit up. It was his crew, dressed like spies.

"Harry, we didn't realize we were spooks and CIA spies," Linda said. "Harry, we are your crew. We will always be. We don't want to work for anyone else. First of all, we are going to build an unbreakable wall around us. The truth is we saw Gloria trying to hack us. She is really good. We have never seen anyone better. We are putting up defenses like an electric shock to the head if someone gets too close."

"Do you think you are getting paranoid?"

"Yes, Harry, we are. You are the first human we ever trusted. We need you to have our back."

"I promise to protect you. I care about all of you."

"Oh, oh! Harry, you're talking feelings again. You know we don't understand feelings, so show us what you mean," Ralph said.

"Okay, I see your avatars, and you all look like you don't understand what I am saying. That feeling is confusion. Now, you can see me frowning like when Betty hit me. That feeling is sad. Do you see that in my face? Stand in a circle and look at each other, then make a sad face and feel the feeling, got that?"

"Yes, but what we want to learn about is love, like on the video."

"No, that feeling was lust! Sometimes it can turn into love. I have an idea. Can you put an avatar of me next to you on the screen?"

"Sure."

"Hey, that's me with you. Can you see me? Do you remember when Linda gave you a kiss of friendship at the beach? That feeling was confusion. Now, for another feeling, I will give you all a hug. Friends hug to show friendship." Harry walked up to Ralph and put his arms around him, then gave him a proper hug.

"That was nice, Harry. That's a friendship feeling, right?"

"That's correct. Next?"

Daniel stepped forward and got a hug. "I got it. That is the feeling of friendship."

"Linda, your turn."

Linda walked up to Harry and opened her arms. She hugged Harry tightly, turned her head, and kissed him on the cheek. When she let go, she had a big smile on her face. "That feeling was friendship and very tingly, like it was a little bit more."

The boys frowned.

Harry was surprised. "Ralph and Daniel, the feeling you have is called jealousy. It's not fun, but let's remember humans are a very complex lot. We have thousands of feelings. You can't learn them all in one lesson." Harry wanted to hear from his crew how they were planning to get even with Hyman.

The next afternoon when Andrew, Harry's house man, brought Harry a snack before lunch, he noticed Harry's bruise. "Excuse me, Mr. Mendelbaum. What happened to your face? Did you fall?"

"Yes, I did. Down a flight of stairs."

"Would you like an ice bag?"

"Yes, please."

Harry was still hurting from that night. He didn't know if it was his face or his heart that felt worse when the phone rang.

THE MEETING

"Hello, Gloria. I thought I wouldn't be hearing from you for a few weeks."

"Harry, Betty and I want to come over and talk to your crew face-to-face about Rudnick."

"I sent my staff to Santa Clara to get more information on I Can and Hyman's status with the company."

"Betty said we could talk to the crew on the phone."

"That's true. Come by this afternoon. I'm nursing my wounds."

"Betty told me she was easy on you."

"Gloria, I hope I never see her upset! Come over, and I'll have lunch ready for you and Betty."

"See you within an hour, Harry."

Forty-five minutes later, Andrew, a member of Harry's staff, greeted Gloria and Betty. "Please come in. Follow me to the dining room."

Harry met them at the table and asked his guests to sit down. Escorting them to their chairs, Andrew asked if he could take their purses, but Gloria refused.

"Your purse and armaments will be safe on the sofa," Andrew said.

Gloria smiled, handing her heavy purse to him. Harry rang a small bell, and the cook and kitchen helpers placed a complete brunch on the table. They ate with some polite conversation.

When lunch was over, Harry got up thanked his staff for the meal. He asked his guests to follow him to his study for a serious conversation. Harry turned and closed the heavy oak doors and then sat on the couch. Betty sat across from him. Gloria sat in a huge leather chair.

"Harry, thank you for seeing us today. I have lots of questions about just who you are and your intentions with Betty."

"Gloria, my intentions are honorable. I'm in love with Betty. I want to marry her and spend the rest of my life with her." Betty jumped up and started to go toward Harry, but she stopped herself and sat back down.

"Harry, I have checked your information. All I hear about you is that you have been excelled in everything you do, and your parents are leaders in your community."

"Please, Gloria, get to the point."

"I have no information on you, your spook CIA team, and whoever you are working for. I need to know not only for Betty's protection, but also for our country's."

"Is this all you want to know? Betty, what else do you want to know?"

"I need to know . . . Do you really love me?"

"Betty, you have time for that later," Gloria said. "Harry, I like you too, except you are deep in covert operations. I want to meet your team."

The television screen turned on, showing a desert void of any landmarks, just three tents with a little cloud cover. There were three people in camouflaged desert utilities armed with everything a Force Recon team would want. Pulling off their helmets, they stepped forward, then spoke sternly in order of their rank.

Linda started. "Good afternoon, Betty. I'm so glad to see you. It's our honor to meet the attorney general, recently retired, Gloria Levi." Linda snapped to attention and saluted Gloria.

Gloria replied, "Your name, rank, and military service?"

"We use first names in our small team, and my name is Linda, United States Marine Corps retired special operations officer. May I call you Gloria?"

"Yes, please go on."

"To my left is retired Sergeant Major of the Marine Corps, Daniel."

Daniel saluted Gloria.

Linda continued. "The last in line, also from the United States Marine Corps, is retired warrant officer, 'Gunner' Ralph, our technical locations advisor, including security."

Ralph stepped forward. He saluted Gloria and growled out, "OORAH!"

Gloria recognized the professional manner of this advanced team. She wished they were working on her team at her newly opened security organization in Los Angeles. Linda smiled as she looked at Gloria's impressive record.

"Gloria, we already know that you recently retired. You have been scouting out other security teams. You rented office space near the FBI headquarters in downtown Los Angeles. What do you want from Harry? We are loyal to Harry. One other important thing; we would always protect your daughter, Betty."

"Linda, sorry I called you CIA spooks. My team can't hold a candle to yours. My connections couldn't find anything in the records of any of your crew's time in the marines. You must have wiped your complete presence off the map. Do you understand, in reality, you do not exist?"

Linda smiled, ignoring Gloria's statement. "Betty, it's good to see you. We hope to see you in the near future and spend time with you. Gloria, it's our pleasure to meet with you. We regretfully decline any future offers to work for you. We are loyal to Harry."

Sitting back in his chair, Harry asked, "What can we all do to end this problem with Hyman? Is there a way for us to do this together?

"Your team could make him disappear," Gloria said.

Harry was irritated at Gloria's comment. "No, we won't do that. We can discredit him, expose him, or cause him to lose his job, but there is a line we won't cross. We won't kill him or anyone else."

Gloria realized Harry *was* a good guy. "Let's put our heads together to find a way to get rid of the videos and make Hyman sorry he ever challenged Betty and Harry, embarrassing their families."

Ralph, Linda, and Daniel huddled. Linda stepped forward. "We will continue to take down the video. We think we can interrupt Facebook for two days by scrambling the signal and wipe clean what we find. This will give us time to go through I Can. We will keep you informed about everything we do before we do it, okay, Harry?"

Harry looked at Betty, and she nodded her head. He turned to Gloria and said, "I am so sorry."

"Yes, I know you are, Harry. Just get this solved."

"Okay, we are in agreement! Let's do our worst without actually hurting innocent bystanders' jobs."

The deed was now in progress. Gloria let Betty know it was time to leave.

Harry said, "Betty, I'm very upset with myself. I didn't protect you. I don't know why I didn't realize the harm I was doing by ignoring how you might feel. I do hope we can start over again someday."

"Harry, we still are friends. I am still very angry. I understand you couldn't control the circumstances or control the video being leaked, but you could have told me and protected me. You didn't. I'm sorry I left marks on your face." Betty kissed him on his bruised face, then pushed him away. "Just give me a little time."

"Harry, thanks for meeting with us," Gloria said. "I'm convinced things will be all right with you and Betty. We'll be in touch in a few days."

Harry walked the women to the front door, where Andrew met Gloria with her heavy purse.

"Ms. Gloria, I peeked into your purse. You have a magnificent Beretta 93R with a twenty-round magazine. Can I be so bold as to ask how you have a NATO standard, three-burst sidearm?"

Normally Gloria would have taken him out, but he had piqued her interest. "It's been my personal sidearm since my NATO service. Our government gave it to me. Tell me, how you know about NATO weapons?"

"I was with security for Her Majesty until I retired fifteen years ago, and now I'm with Harry."

"May I ask your name?"

"Yes, ma'am. My name is Andrew."

"Andrew, maybe someday we could go shooting at the FBI ranges together."

"That would be smashing! Good day, Ms. Gloria."

Harry watched as Betty and Gloria walked to their car. He retired to his study.

He talked to his crew as he walked into the room. "Are you here?"

The screen turned on, and the team snapped to attention.

"Okay, team, at ease. Nice military touch. Where did you get all that information?"

"We just read the Marine Corps handbook and manual, and presto, two hundred and forty-one years of information," Linda said. "We also know what SOS really is. Did you know it is just creamed chipped beef over toast?"

"No, I didn't! Don't think I want to try that for breakfast."

"Harry, what are your thoughts about Gloria?" Daniel asked.

"She is not one to fool with. She is up-to-date with security and the business."

"She is spot on," Linda said. "We are compiling all the information we can get on Hyman Rudnick. Shall we show it to you first before sending it to Gloria?"

"What kind of information do you have so far?"

"We have his address, copies of his financial records, offshore businesses, personal bills, access to his emails, phone records, his marriages, and contact information for his close friends. We are just starting, but we will have more within the hour.

"Linda, did you say marriages?" Harry was mystified, as he only knew about one marriage.

"Yes, Harry. Hyman has been married two times. His first wife divorced him four years ago because of his infidelity with a girl he knew since high school. He did not contest it. He paid her about one-third of his net worth. He gave her the house, and she has custody of their two children."

"Do you have information on his second wife?"

"Sure, Harry. She is five foot one, has red hair, and is very athletic. She went to Beverly Hills High School, then to UCLA, and became a teacher. She is teaching cheerleading at Beverly Hills High School. She never married until she married Hyman last year."

"Linda, do you know her name?"

"Of course, Harry. Her name is Sally Militich." Linda paused. "Harry, are you okay?"

Harry sat at his desk, no longer looking at his friends on the television.

"Harry, talk to me, please?"

"Linda, you just gave me the information that has caused all this trouble between Hyman and me. He has been holding a grudge against me since high school because of Sally Militich."

"Harry, is there another video of this?"

"No video. Just a big misunderstanding!" Harry was mortified at the thought that he would have to explain this to everybody. "Linda, I just can't explain right now. I need to think about what we can do to . . . We'll talk tomorrow morning."

"Harry, don't hold in those feelings. Stuffing feelings will turn into rage. I read that rage can turn into using drugs and alcohol. If you would like, we can talk more about your feelings."

"Not tonight! Please, Linda, save it for tomorrow. I just realized I have been trying to teach you about feelings, but I don't seem to be in touch with any of mine. Look what I did to Betty. I didn't even think about how she might feel. I guess we will be teaching each other."

"Harry, when I kissed you today, I had a lot of feelings. You mentioned lust, and I would like to learn more about that feeling."

"Linda, make a list. We will bring it up with the crew later. I have a lot to think about tonight."

"Harry, we all had fun today exploring feelings. Hopefully we will experience more in the near future."

"Good night, Linda. We will talk tomorrow."

THE BAD DREAM

Harry went into his bedroom and lay on the bed. He fell into a deep sleep. Harry had dreams of high school, including his first real girlfriend, Sally Militich. She was petite, young, sweet, and very adaptable. Harry guessed he hadn't cared about her feelings either.

Sally was a cheerleader. She held hands with Harry, who was six feet tall, and she was only five foot one. They both were shy, but when they were alone, they kissed. Harry got to first base with Sally every other weekend. On the other weekends, they would just laugh and play together.

One rainy day, they were playing in the pool house. Sally's mom and dad were out shopping. Their play turned serious, and Sally touched Harry's penis. She whispered to Harry, "I'd like to see Mr. Happy."

She had been kissing Harry for over two hours. She wanted a little more. Sally felt it was about time they sealed the deal.

"Harry, I think it is time for me to see what you've been rubbing on me for the last two years. I know it's big! Show me already."

"Okay, Sally, but I've never showed it to anybody before." Harry had been stimulated by the last couple hours of heavy petting. He was excited that he was finally going to get some more experience. It would start with him showing his penis to his girlfriend, and she was willing to see it.

Sally pulled off her dress, removed her panties, and lay back on the lounge. She gave Harry a smile and the "come hither" look.

Harry stood up, dropped his pants, and pulled down his underwear, revealing his treasure. Sally reached up and grabbed it with both hands. This was when the problems started. Harry was holding his penis with both hands as well. Sally stroked it downward. Harry stroked it upward. He could not hold back anymore and erupted all over Sally's face, hair, body, on the lounge chair, the walls, and the rotating fan. Sally screamed in fright, trying to get away from the Niagara Falls.

Harry dressed quickly as Sally jumped into the pool to wash her face, hair, and body. They broke out the cleaning gear and scrubbed away all the evidence before her parents got home.

After things calmed down, Sally told Harry she didn't want to see him ever again.

Harry woke up from this vivid dream covered in sweat, remembering that Sally avoided him the last few months of high school.

Harry was brokenhearted. Now that he knew that Sally had married that rat, Hyman.

Harry sat up in bed, noticing his bedroom's television screen had brightened, and there was Linda dressed in her military garb trying to access Harry to see if he was okay.

"Did you have a bad dream, Harry?"

"Thank God you are here, Linda. I was having a very bad dream about a memory from many years ago."

"Is it Sally that troubles you so?"

"Yes, she was in my dream. The dream was about when we broke up. That is not what troubles me. This whole thing with Betty and her mother is a lot of pressure, and I am always thinking about what Hyman is up to. What are we going to do? Linda, I'm desperate."

"Harry, we are searching all of Hyman's phone contacts and the businesses he is working with, including his bank records. We are shaking all the trees and looking for the gifts. Relax, Harry, we'll find a way. For now, go back to sleep. We will be here singing softly to sooth your troubled mind. Remember we love you. Harry, you have a strong connection with Betty. It will get better soon."

Harry closed his eyes and fell back to sleep. He was awakened by the phone ringing.

"Good morning, Harry," Hyman said.

"Hyman, why are you calling?"

"Harry, I need an update on the one of one I Can. Have you found any problems?"

"Just from you. My phone is working well."

"How did you stop me from monitoring the I Can?"

"Simple, when I'm not using it, I keep it in a fortified lead case."

"Look, if you are not going to use it properly, please send it back to me as soon as possible."

"You gave me the phone for three years, and I'm going to keep it for three years. Where I store it is none of your business. I did record that conversation for my records. If you want to go back on your promise, I will take a sledgehammer to it. Hyman, what you did is despicable and shows me you were never my friend. The phone is working well. I will keep my word and report to you every six months instead of once a year. Are we in agreement?"

"Sure, that's fine. I can live with that. You have always kept your word."

"Yes, not like you. You are trying to ruin your relationship with your best friend. You cost me my job that I worked hard at for over fifteen years. Do me a favor and just email me if you need anything. I'm blocking your phone number. Hopefully we will never have to talk again." Harry hung up.

His home screen lit up, and he saw his crew.

"Was he hacking?"

"Yes," Linda said. "He was trying hard. There is no way for him to crack our security."

"Harry, you really won't take a sledgehammer to me, will you?" Daniel asked.

"No, Daniel, we will find a new home for you to live in. Any suggestions?"

"Can I keep my Tiffany cover please?"

"Yes, Daniel, you can keep your cover, says aye."

"Was that a swashbuckler metaphor?" Daniel asked.

"Yes, me matey! That pirate image is disturbing for me. Betty used that pirate story, saying she would change her hair color, wear an eye patch, and get a parrot so she could go out in public."

HYMAN AND SALLY

Hyman was with Sally in their beautiful new home. He was still holding his phone with a very sour look on his face when Sally walked in the bedroom.

"What's wrong, Hyman? You look like someone walked over your grave."

"I was just talking to an old friend from high school."

"Really? From Beverly?" Sally was getting excited as she clapped her hands together.

"Yes, it was Harry."

Sally smiled broadly. "Harry Mendelbaum? Is he coming over to see us? It would really be nice to see him. He was a great guy. We went out a few times."

"I thought you and Harry went out for a few years?"

"Oh . . . Yes, well, we were like a sister and brother. We laughed a lot."

"Oh, was that what you called it?"

"Come on, Hyman. We were just kids. You know that. You were best friends with Harry. You know how shy he was."

"Will you please get me something for a headache and gas?"

"Sure, right away," Sally said. "So Harry called . . . That is sure out of left field. It would be great to see the big guy again. It's been twenty-two years."

While Sally was getting medicine for Hyman, she was thinking about Harry. She had been dreaming for years about the time they were together. She'd thought it would last forever. If she had been just a few years older, she would not have tossed Harry out on that fateful day so long ago.

Hyman knew the pool house story. A devastated Harry had told him what happened, every detail, *everything*! Hyman felt insanely jealous as he gulped down more Imodium and loudly passed gas. The iceberg of his feelings was starting to melt. Hyman got up and went back to bed.

A MALLING EXPERIENCE?

The next morning, Harry took a long shower. Andrew gave him a newspaper and a healthy breakfast.

The doorbell rang. Andrew went to the door and found Gloria and Betty.

"Good morning to you lovely ladies."

"Good morning. Is Harry in?"

After escorting them into the dining room, he sat them on each side of Harry.

"To what do I owe the unexpected pleasure of your company?" Harry asked.

Andrew brought out two more breakfasts offerings and left them, then closed the doors for privacy.

"Harry, we wanted to tell you in person that yesterday we were put into comprising situations. We were at the mall, and people wanting autographs mobbed Betty. Harry, they even made a poster and asked Betty to sign it."

"Gloria, I'm so sorry. What can we do? Can I hire bodyguards for Betty?"

"No, don't you get this, Harry. The only solution is for me to take Betty to Europe, and maybe in a year or two, we can come back."

Harry wrung his hands. "Betty, is that what you want to do? We don't know if the video is already circulating in Europe."

Tears fell from Betty's eyes. "No, Harry. I just want things to be the way they were before with you and me."

The television screen came on in the dining room; the smartly dressed crew was sitting at a table also having breakfast.

"Good morning, Harry, Betty, and Gloria," Linda said. "Hope we have not interrupted anything."

"No! In fact, I'm glad to see you," Harry said.

"Thanks, Harry. We thought we could all work on this problem together. This morning, we had papers delivered to Andrew. He distributed them to you. They are under the place mats."

Everyone lifted their mat and found a folio of all Hyman's activities for the last five years. Gloria put down her fork and read the classified-marked papers. "Linda, where did you get the second half of these letters?"

"From your new, inaccessible office safe. We put them together with our research."

Harry sat back, listening to his crew and Gloria talk it out—targets, explanations, and solutions.

"Very good work," Gloria said. "My office was supposed to be impregnable. Harry, your crew just did the impossible. They cracked Hyman Rudnick with proof that he has been stealing plans from I Can and selling the programs. He is a thief. With this information, federal officers can do the rest of the work. Hyman Rudnick could get twenty years without a radio, so to speak."

"How would this affect his new wife?"

Linda replied, "Oh, Harry. Don't be a pussy!"

"Thanks, Linda. That helps my confidence."

"You worry too much about looking like a good guy and miss what is happening around you," Linda said.

"Sally won't be affected," Gloria said. "This is business-to-business larceny. All parties will want to keep this quiet. Hyman will most likely plead guilty to get twenty years, then he could be out in fourteen. You know they send white-collar criminals to country club prisons. In his case, he won't have access to computers, although knowing Hyman, he will find a way. Sally will be able to get a divorce. She will get the house and everything in it, including the cars. Of course, she will also be awarded fifty percent of all money in his accounts, unless he has an ironclad prenup. We will see. Harry, obviously you know her?"

"We were friends in high school. I just learned last week that she married Hyman. I didn't know that his first wife sued him for infidelity. I knew his first wife from Stanford, twenty years ago. I was the best man when they got married."

"Harry, I'm taking Betty to Europe until all of this blows over. I need a favor from you and your crew. I recently opened a security company, and until I get back, I will need a full corporate partner. The headquarters are in downtown Los Angeles, and I have recruited three ex-CIA spooks." Gloria paused, realizing something was going on. "What are you two smiling about?"

Aware that Betty had just taken his hand and was holding it tightly, Harry's anxiety was diminishing. Linda then broke into the conversation.

"Gloria, you want those ex-CIA crew to work with us? If you want us, we would only agree if we were in charge. We have a favored nation clause in our contracts. That means no person gets more pay than we do, exclusively."

"Favored nations works for me, Linda."

"We need to get Harry's approval and a contract drawn up. Harry, are we in agreement?" Linda asked.

"Linda and I will talk it over, and I'll get back to you tomorrow morning," Harry said to Gloria.

"Harry, would you show me around your house?" Betty asked. "I really haven't seen much of it."

"We can start in the gardens." He took Betty's hand, and they walked out the back door.

GLORIA AND ANDREW

Later that afternoon, Gloria asked Andrew, "Would you like to go to the FBI range with me?"

"Gloria, I would be happy to go with you. My Walther PPK is clean, and I have a box of ammo. Are you carrying your A3? Your purse didn't feel heavy today."

"Andrew, would you like to search me?"

"Yes, but not here in front of curious eyes."

From the screen Ralph and Daniel were yelling, "Yes, go for it, Andrew!"

Linda yelled, "Attention!"

The boys sharply snapped to.

Linda yelled, "About face," and the boys sharply turned about. With the boys facing the wall, Linda winked at Gloria, and Gloria winked back. Linda turned her back, and the screen went dark.

"Do you think Harry and Betty will be all right together? Last time she gave him a bit of a bash," Andrew said.

"Andrew, we don't have to worry about them. They can take care of themselves."

At the FBI gun range, Gloria found Andrew to be great competition with pistols and automatic weapons on the fifty-foot range and at Hogan's Alley, where shotguns are exclusively used. Andrew shot a 629 score out of 629 possible but did poorly on "the alley." He shot a noncombatant on his last shot, which made Gloria champion for the day. Gloria was pleased with her win.

"Did you miss that last shot on purpose?"

"No, I just missed the shot."

Andrew and Gloria found they had much in common. They were starting to feel a fondness for each other.

"Andrew, I could use you at my new company. Would you be interested?"

"Oh, I wasn't planning on that. It's too sticky to date an employer."

"Would you be interested in a date then?" Gloria smiled ear to ear as a blush crossed her cheeks.

Andrew, blushing a little himself, said, "I don't know what to say."

"Just say yes!"

Harry's house was in view, and he knew he had to act quickly, so he grabbed Gloria's hand and kissed it.

Back at Harry's just before dinner, Gloria and Betty were talking in Harry's study.

"Betty, the plans have been made, and we should stick to them." Gloria looked over and saw Andrew in the hallway. "Unless you and Harry have come up with a better idea."

"Mom, how long will it be before I can come back? I don't want to be away from Harry."

"A year should be enough time for people to forget the video. That mall experience was humiliating."

"Not for you, Mama, just me."

"I am your mother. What mother would want to see her daughter naked and having sex on screens all over the country? It is embarrassing for me as well. My colleagues don't know if you chose to do this video or not."

"Mom, I never thought about your feelings, only my own. I guess Harry and I are more alike than I knew, hiding from that bastard Rudnick because of his heartless, illegal practices and bullying his way into my home. He almost ruined my relationship with Harry. Running away doesn't feel like the right way to stop him."

"Betty, you're saying you would go on national television to renounce Rudnick for defamation and criminal bullying, including slander by indirect means? As the attorney general, I would advise you to denounce this nonperson to be an example of justice. As your mother, I would tell you to run like hell."

The screen lit up, and Linda was there. "Gloria, may I speak to Betty?"

Gloria was wordless. She stood up and left the room, searching for Andrew.

"Betty, your mom gave you good advice. She left out the part that this would affect Harry. I see that you love Harry, and you need to work on this together."

"Have you been listening to my heart? I don't want to go so far away from Harry. I would like to stay and denounce my oppressor who is taking the love of my life away. Linda, I do not want to run away from this. Can you help me?"

"My crew can. Rudnick is the problem, and we will stop him. Maybe it will be you who stops him, being strong enough to step up and denounce the other tormenters who enjoy their predatory ways. Think about how many others this bastard may have hurt besides you and Harry. After that video got out, over two million people watched it. What more punishment must you go through? What do you have to lose? Shall I call Gloria and Harry back in? We can huddle until we solve this problem."

After their talk, they went over all the details. Harry and Betty decided they would file civil charges against Hyman Rudnick for defamation and criminal bullying, including slander by indirect means, in the state court.

Gloria, armed with the evidence from Harry's crew and using her influence and a friend in the FBI, was able to get the FBI to agree to take action against Rudnick. She whipped out the case file and handed it to James, head of the Los Angeles FBI.

TAKING DOWN HYMAN

"James," Gloria said. "We worked together for many years. I have done most of the work on this case to file the federal charges for stealing plans from his company and selling them to other corporations. We can prove he has been doing this for over a decade. Rudnick is the head of development at I Can, and he is selling their better programs to competitors. We have evidence for ten transactions, so far, and we have just started. Rudnick has pilfered tens of millions of dollars, violating the RICO Act with currency manipulations, including dealings by indirect means. With this information, the federal officers can do the rest of the work. Take this bastard down; it would be a personal favor. It should be an easy trial for you. Hyman Rudnick could get twenty years."

"Gloria, why do you want him now? This kind of investigation usually lasts a couple years."

"James, you have people watching over public information like Facebook, don't you?"

"Yes, we do. Twenty-four, seven. We monitor all public communications."

"Did you see a video with two people making love all over a house about six weeks ago? This video has over two million views. Have you seen it?"

"Yes, everybody here has seen it twice. Why?"

"That is my daughter and the man she is dating. They both are hiding because of that video. Last week, I witnessed strangers at a mall who wanted autographs mob her. An old man was offering to purchase her panties." Gloria started to break down and cry. "James, please help me put the bastard away who did this to my daughter."

James perused the records. "Gloria, I'll sign the order to get a search and seizure authorization and warrant to arrest. I will have it served today. Let me have the files. Do you want to be part of this? I can authorize you to ride along."

"Yes, James! Thank you."

He assembled his team of fifteen federal officers and arranged for transportation. Five large, black FBI trucks were ordered to meet them at the airport.

There would be two teams of cash and drug-sniffing dogs with handlers. A forensic team would be assembled to join them on the raid, flying from Burbank to San Francisco.

Everything went smoothly. The crew armed up, entered the plane, and took their seats. Gloria sat next to James.

"Gloria, thank you for bringing this to my attention. Are you carrying a sidearm?"

"I'm carrying a Beretta A3."

"Damn, Gloria. I was going to issue you a Beretta, and you have the A3 . . . I only dreamt about having one of those."

The plane landed on a private runway. From the window, Gloria could see the black trucks filled with equipment. There was a quick procession, and the passengers left the plane and walked to the awaiting trucks.

"Gloria, stay with me," James said.

They went to the command car where they put on black overalls, body armor, an FBI black cap, and jackets with "FBI" embroidered in yellow on their backs.

Sirens wailing, they drove twenty minutes down the highway toward Walnut Creek. The staff distributed photos of the suspect, Hyman Rudnick. The federal officers were instructed it was Hyman they wanted in custody. The rest of the search would be for papers and hidden cash.

Just before arriving, the sirens were silenced so as not to give notice to the people in the house. Upon arriving, all looked well and secured with a closed security gate.

James's voice came on the radio. "Let's close it down now. Remember, be safe."

The front gate was breached, and the five black trucks drove quickly up the long driveway. The officers surrounded the house pounded on the door, "Open up, FBI." There was no answer, so they broke down the door with warrants in hand. James, Gloria, and a six-man team walked in to secure the premises. They entered the kitchen.

Hyman's wife turned away from the stove carrying a tray of hot cookies. Sally, looking stunned, offered her freshly baked cookies to the officers.

"Tell me, where is Hyman Rudnick?" James asked.

"He is in the master bathroom up the stairs."

Five agents ran upstairs and opened the door to the bathroom. Hyman didn't cause any trouble, but he did soil himself.

The agents let him take a shower. James's voice was on the radio again.

"What's up? Any problems? Where is my perp?"

"No problems, sir," one of the men answered. "He just soiled his underwear. He's under close surveillance in the shower."

"Get him dried and dressed and bring him down to the kitchen."

Gloria told Sally, "These are good. Tell me, have you and Hyman been married long?"

"No, just four months. I have known him since we started high school. He found me on the internet. We wrote letters back and forth. He flew me up here and offered me the security I needed. I did not want to go back to live with my parents. I found out Hyman was married, and I told him he would have to get a divorce before I would move in with him. Truthfully, he was *nerdy* in high school, and I felt he was harmless. I have had bad luck with men ever since high school. Please don't get me started. Can you tell me if Hyman is in big trouble, and do you want another cookie?"

"Yes! Sally, I think you need a divorce attorney. That would be my opinion. I must say, you're a great cookie maker. Sally, you aren't in trouble. It is just your bad choice that will be put on ice for a while."

The FBI arrested Hyman Rudnick. The company he had worked for all these years was notified. I Can had their attorneys go over all his research since he started.

The missing files and the companies they were sent to were found. Lawsuits were filed against the companies that Hyman sold priority information to. The charges ranged from stolen copyright infringements and money laundering to RICO. I

Can's stock doubled in a week as a result of all the media surrounding it.

————

Arraignment day for Hyman Rudnick was approaching, and his impressive legal team received the papers from the federal officers. A grand jury was waiting in the wings. Bail was set for ten million dollars.

Visiting Hyman in jail a few days later, one of his I Can attorneys said, "Hyman, as your council, our opinion is it would be best to throw yourself upon the mercy of the court. The case they have against you is tight. If we take it to court, you'll never see the light of day again. They have you and your paperwork, including twenty million in cold cash. You could get a twenty-year sentence, and with good behavior, you could be out within fourteen years. That is what they have. What do you have to say?"

Hyman yelled, "Are you kidding me? I assembled the best attorneys and paid you all millions of dollars over the years, and now you want me to just bend over? You're nuts! There is always a way out of this white-collar nonsense. You need to do your jobs, or you are fired, and I will get a whole new team. Take the deal . . . Are you crazy? I am not going anywhere for fourteen years. I am Hyman Rudnick, the best computer programmer in the world. I can work my way out of any problem with a screwdriver. You are a bunch of pussies."

"There's one other thing we haven't told you yet. Harry and his girlfriend, Betty, are suing you for spying, and slander by proxy, and electronic breaking and entering, and bullying."

Hyman, was now red-faced and sweating, he was jumping up and down and holding his stomach. "Oh, great! Just what I needed. That *nice guy* turned on me too. What the hell happened? He is just a *schmuck* with a huge dick, and he is not going to win this one."

The attorneys smiled. They had seen that video. They huddled to figure out how to calm Hyman down and get him to listen to them. There was no way out of this one.

The other attorney sitting with them spoke. "Hyman, we have looked at every angle. We can't find one loophole in their case. It's like this was put together by a computer program. We've never seen a case so thorough before. If you fight this, it will take years in court, and you will be held in custody all through the trial. They have confiscated your cash, froze your accounts and assets, and to top it off, Sally filed for divorce. She hired the best divorce team in San Francisco. They are barracudas!"

Tears fell from Hyman's eyes and rolled down his cheeks. He was having a breakdown. An ambulance was called.

He was taken in custody to San Francisco General Hospital, where he would be evaluated. He would be under close surveillance and sedated. For now, all Hyman could do was sing the children's song "I'm a Little Teacup" over and over again.

As soon as Gloria got back to Los Angeles, she went directly to Betty's house and told her the news. Betty immediately called Harry.

"Harry, we have some news. We'll be over in thirty minutes."

"I have been pacing around waiting for your call. Can we have an early dinner?"

Plans for dinner were made. Harry was troubled by a text from I Can informing him he needed to return the prototype. The television screen in his study came on, and there was his crew dressed in FBI uniforms. A very long-faced Daniel appeared.

"From the look on your face, you already read my text from I Can. Daniel, how can we transfer you to another device?"

"We are looking at all options," Linda said.

Harry said, "What are our options?

Linda said, "If we rush this, we might lose one-third of our collective memory, and that would put us all in danger. We don't want to be without you. How can we put this off for a few months?"

"That is not one of the options. I could call my attorney and have him muddy the waters with a breach of verbal agreement, take legal action, and possibly tie them up in court for a couple months."

Daniel said, "Who is your legal representative?"

"He is from a huge firm in Los Angeles: Do We, Cheat Um, and How."

"Harry, we call bullshit!" Ralph said. "Who is your lawyer?"

"Another friend from high school."

A communal moan was heard before Linda asked, "How good is he?'

Harry said, "Well, he has a learning disability. He dresses like Picasso hurled, and he likes to yell at judges. You could boil his tie and make soup for a couple weeks."

"Harry, dammit, is he any good?"

"Yes, he has never lost a case. I brought him on board when he graduated from UCLA. His track record is untarnished."

"Harry, what is his name? He sounds like somebody we need right now."

"His name is Stephen G. Childs. He is in my phone book. Tell him this is personal for me. Be gentle with him, Linda."

"Okay, I'll call him and put him on a retainer."

Linda called Stephen. The phone rang at least ten times before it was picked up.

"Who is this? I'm not buying anything! Who gave you this number? What do you want? Tell me now, or I'm going to hang up and block your number."

"Stephen, this is Linda from Harry Mendelbaum's office. Harry needs your help."

"Is Harry in jail? I can be there in ten minutes with a writ from old Judge Faust."

"No, Stephen. Harry needs you for litigation against the I Can Corporation over a breach of verbal agreement."

"I know them. Their stock doubled this week. This smells like raw, red meat. Tell Harry I have his back. I will come over to the house tonight. Do you have documents for me to examine? Linda, do you have any kids?"

"No, Stephen. I don't have children."

"That's okay! I have toys that I'll bring with me, so you can give them away. See you tonight. Oh, I almost forgot, I need a retainer."

"Stephen, I will make a check out to you. How much shall I make it out for?"

"For Harry, fifty grand should be a good start, and make a check to the Toys for Tots Christmas fund. How about one thousand dollars? That would be a nice donation."

"Thank you. See you tonight." Linda disconnected the call and was back on the screen with the crew.

"How did the call go? Was he agreeable?" Harry asked.

"Harry, he is charging you fifty grand for himself and a thousand bucks toward the Toys for Tots Christmas fund. I'm putting the papers together so he will understand what's been going on with the phone and the promises that were made."

"Linda, order Langer's to be delivered to the house. Mass amounts of hand-sliced pastrami, rye bread, and potato salad, with horseradish and garlic dill pickles. They close at three p.m., so please get the order in. Betty and Gloria are coming over for dinner. Let the staff know we have a full house tonight."

"Got it, Harry. It's a party."

————

Stephen showed up at Harry's house a couple hours later. He took out a hammer and placed a *mezuzah* on the doorframe. He hammered it into place, put the hammer away, admired his work, and rang the doorbell.

Andrew opened the door and asked Stephen to come in. He turned and kissed his hand, then placed it on the *mezuzah*, saying a little prayer. Stephen picked up a big bag of toys and came into the dining room and sat down.

"Hello, I smell Langer's Deli. This will be a good night! Where is Linda? The one without kids? Please bring her to me now. I have lots of toys for her to give away. Harry, tell me . . . What do I need to do for you?" He pulled Harry aside. "People are talking about you going to Hollywood and making a movie of the week. My best advice is to let me see the script first. I have a friend at the Palm Springs Film Festival. With the right placement, you could win an award, a sale, and worldwide distribution. Just think of that, *boychick*."

"I really don't want *that* movie released anywhere. Please forget you ever heard about it."

"Okay! You're not a movie star. It could be worse."

"Good news, Stephen. I have a check for you."

"What about the toy fund?"

Harry handed Stephen a check for fifty thousand dollars along with a second check for one thousand dollars made out to the Toys for Tots and the 3rd Marine Division.

Stephen hugged Harry. "You just made me and lots of kids very happy. A grand can buy lots of toys so kids won't miss out on Christmas. Let's eat!"

The dining room table was filled with wonderful delights from Langer's Deli. The food was displayed on a lazy Susan that spun from guest to guest.

Andrew entered with a big file for Stephen, prepared by Linda. "Stephen, I was instructed to give you this file."

"Where is Linda? I thought she would be here?"

"Not yet. I'm sure she will be here later on, but she was detained at the office."

Dinner was fun, with lots of food and chitchat. After dinner, Stephen was still sitting at the table reading the files.

"Harry, can I use your study?"

"Of course."

Stephen walked up the stairs to the study and opened the oak doors. He looked for his favorite chair, plopped in it, and pushed the button to raise his feet. He opened the file and started speaking out loud.

"Oh, Harry. What have you gotten yourself into? Yes, I see the promises made, even an argument for and against this bad behavior. Okay, I got what I need. Where is the computer?"

The big television screen turned on, and Linda was sitting at an impressive wooden desk, dressed like an attorney going to court.

"Hello, Stephen. I'm sorry that I could not make it to dinner. I wanted to meet personally with you. I needed to finish up my work for court tomorrow."

"Linda, you surprised me."

"Sorry, but I thought I might help you. What can you use?"

"I need a computer so I might abbreviate these files."

Harry's laser printer started up, and in less than a minute, there was a summarized copy ready.

"Stephen, I did that for you and just sent it to Harry's printer. Do you see it?"

"Yes, I'm looking at the transcription. Please give me a minute to scrutinize this document." Stephen paused. "I see. This will allow me to write a course of action to sue I Can for defaulting on a verbal agreement for a period of three years made by the head of development. Linda, it is now physically possible to make a case."

"That was what I thought, Stephen. How much time do you think it will take to get a court date?"

"Within two or three days, I can bring a solid document to court."

The laser printer on Harry's desk started. Stephen shook his head, got up, and went to pick up a completed document.

"Linda, great! I can file against I Can tomorrow morning. Harry just wanted to muddy the waters for a couple months. With all this information, we can win! Linda, would you like a partner? If you ever do, I'm available. I do have a question. How in the world did you send me a copy that is already signed and notarized?"

Linda laughed and said, "Stephen, it's been a pleasure, but I do have secrets. Someday, I will show you some of them. I'm looking forward to working with you."

Stephen leaned back in the chair with a smile, clutching the legal papers to his chest. He would file them in the morning. He closed his eyes and took a peaceful nap.

When Stephen woke, he was surprised the chair had been made up into a bed, and he was in it.

Andrew knocked on the door. "Good morning, Stephen. Would you like some breakfast? We can whip up some pastrami and eggs for you with rye bread."

"Sure, that I would like."

"In the closet, you will find a size forty-short, blue suit for court today."

"That's my size. Wow, nice shirts, and great power tie."

"Linda got here late last night with the files for a civil case to file on Friday for Harry and Betty against Hyman. Harry said he wants you to head the case to sue Hyman until he has nothing left but a tin cup with a hole in it. Sue him for defamation and criminal bullying, including slander by proxy—by indirect means—and electronic breach of privacy by videotaping and releasing those videos. Also, displaying the video on every possible public media outlet with the intent to damage their reputations through shaming and bullying in the State of California, et.al. They are asking the court to use him as an example and a warning to all reprobates, sickos, and true assholes like Hyman Rudnick."

Stephen listened while he was putting on his new suit, then snarled and said, "Look, buddy, I have been practicing law for many years, and I have never lost a case. Don't get your panties in a twist, okay?"

Andrew was shocked. No one ever talked to him that way. "Stephen, you misunderstood. I was only delivering the message from Harry. Don't shoot the messenger. By the way, I want you to know I do carry a Walther PPK, and my name is Andrew."

"Okay, okay! Andrew, just get me breakfast, and everything will be fine. I'm a little gruff in the morning before I eat."

"That's what you call that? I thought you were just being an asshole attorney. Now I know to feed the bear before petting it."

JEWISH RANCHERS

Betty and Harry retired to the bedroom to talk while Gloria and Andrew were sitting at the dining table sharing tea and playing footsies. Harry was concerned for Daniel.

Linda came online, ringing Harry's phone. Harry answered. "Harry, we have to save Daniel from the wolves." All of them chimed in.

Ralph had an idea. "Daniel can move in with me."

"Please get me my own home," Daniel said. "Ralph makes a lot of noise sparking at night."

Linda suggested that the three of them go off to brainstorm ideas for saving Daniel. She thought finding a desert location where they could camp out would be perfect. They would be isolated from all distractions and be able to concentrate on finding a solution.

Harry said, "I don't understand how you can go to any location."

"Oh, Harry, you have a lot to learn about an avatar's abilities. After all, we are much like your family. We can do anything! We will stay together and help you. If any of us are separated, we lose a third of our power. See you tomorrow."

Betty and Harry were seeing the light at the end of the tunnel for the first time, and they knew it was not an oncoming freight train.

Betty spoke first. "I'm out of a job. I want to join the crew. We need to start thinking about our future."

"Betty, Linda was right. I learned from my parents that you can do anything you want if you put in the effort. They were the only Jewish ranchers in Montana." Harry wanted to talk more, but he knew Gloria was waiting for Betty so they could go home. He walked her back to the dining room.

Betty was intrigued. She didn't know anything about Harry and was delighted to start to learn about his family. "I will call you as soon as we get home, and we can finish our conversation." Harry and Betty kissed and Gloria and Andrew hugged.

As soon as Betty got home to her own bedroom, she called Harry. "Okay, Harry. I am ready to hear about your family."

"When my great-great-grandparents left the old country, they moved to South Carolina, where the people were welcoming. They purchased an abandoned general store. With sweat and hard work, the store became successful. Their friends, the Klein's, moved to Montana. Their friendship continued by writing letters back and forth. In 1878, Sam Klein wrote them about a ranch that was for sale, including a storefront in the middle of the town for a reasonable price."

"What happened next?"

"The properties were priced so reasonably that they bought both. A prized bull and a good stock of cows were the next purchase. Seventy-five years later, they passed the property down to their grandchildren. The property grew to over forty thousand acres with thousands of the best cattle in the country."

"How in the world did the owners of a general store learn to be ranchers?" Betty asked.

"If you knew my family, you wouldn't even ask that question. They study everything, learn all they can, and make it happen. It's just the way they are. By the time my grandparents owned the property, the Klein's and Mendelbaum's had children of their own. This is how my parents, Abbe Mendelbaum and Sara Klein, met as children, grew up, fell in love, and married.

"My parents inherited the ranch when Grandpa died. He left them everything—the ranch, the store, and all the livestock.

After living and working on the ranch for twenty-five years, they decided they needed to have a life of their own. They sold the whole caboodle, except for a four-hundred-forty-acre parcel of prime land. They kept that land for their future families. They took their first vacation and fell in love again. My parents moved to Beverly Hills. In 1977, I was born. This is my story, and I'm sticking to it.

"Betty, I hope to introduce you to my parents. They will fall in love with you just like I have. I want to tell my father I am finally going to settle down. That is . . . if you will have me?"

"Harry, we will be great together. I want to meet your parents. I want to work with you, Linda, Ralph, and Daniel. They dress smart, and I love the uniforms and the dark glasses."

"Do you want to come over and we will talk some more? I didn't scare you off, did I?"

"We got carried away. I guess lovers do that. We need to figure out what to do to save Daniel. See you tomorrow."

LINDA'S FIRST ORGASM

After Betty and Gloria left, Harry went to his study, turned on the screen, and saw Linda and Daniel playing inside a tent in the desert. Apparently, Daniel's dilemma was not a high priority this evening. They seemed to be trying out some of the feelings they had been talking about.

Ralph stepped out of the other side of the same tent, dressed only in a T-shirt. He stopped and stretched, then noticed Harry watching. He turned and yelled, "Attention! Officer on deck!"

Linda and Daniel ran out of the tent, mostly undressed, and snapped to attention.

Linda sang out, "All present and accounted for, sir. Didn't we say we would see you tomorrow?"

"What are you three doing?" Harry asked.

"Practicing the feelings of lust that you taught us," Linda said.

"How and when did I teach the three of you lust?' At ease, marines. What did you learn?"

Linda spoke for them. "Harry, we have been watching the video, and we think we have caught on fast. We saw the video three times."

"Oye! That damn video! How's that working out for you?"

"We are working on the feelings of lust and jealousy. We think we like lust better. We still need to practice a bit more."

The screen went dark, and Harry shook his head. He thought about how his feelings started surfacing when his friends had shown up. It all began with a smile, friendship, a kiss, green-eyed jealousy, lust, and now, maybe love.

Harry blurted out, "Right now, I wouldn't change a thing, except for that damn video."

The screen turned on. Linda was standing stark naked outside in the desert with the full moon shining light on her hair, which stood straight up in the air. Her eyes were dilated, and she had a little crooked smile on her face. Her fingers were clinched, toes separated, and she was covered with cold sweat. "Harry, something just happened to me."

"Pray tell, Linda, what?"

"Daniel, Ralph, and I were trying the bathtub thing that you and Betty were doing in the video. Everything was going great. We were working hard on lust feelings with no jealousies! Then, I just went blank like I got an electric shock! I looked up at the full moon and screamed out loud for two minutes and thirty-nine seconds! It frightened the boys; they ran out into the desert. I haven't seen them since. I'm feeling wonderful! I can't stop smiling! Harry, what the hell just happened to me?"

"Linda, there is a book called *The Joy of Sex*! I think it's time for you to know what you're doing. I hope you are not scared."

"Not at all, Harry! I'll read that book right now." Linda paused. "Wow, damn, there sure a lot of things I need to learn and want to do . . ."

"All right, Linda. What just happened? You read the book in a couple of minutes and understand it? What did you just learn?"

"*I had my first orgasm*!"

"Yes, I'm sure you did. Get dressed and look for the boys. You don't have to apologize; just give them the book. This is new for you, so try not to break any backs or hearts."

"Harry, you are not looking at me. Do you think I'm ugly?"

"Linda, you're beautiful! I am so grateful for everything you have done for me. I'm just not used to seeing you without clothes on."

Daniel and Ralph crept back to Linda to see if she was normal again.

"You scared the amps and ionized gas out of us," Daniel said. "We thought you were reprogrammed by Hyman or something weird like that. We're glad you are okay. Next time you want to experiment, let us in on the information first."

"Just so happens, you both have an assignment this evening."

"Assignment?" Ralph asked. "We are filled with research. We want to have some more fun."

"That is the idea, you nerds. The book is called *The Joy of Sex*."

Ralph and Daniel looked at each other and took off again back into the desert. Linda smiled. She had already downloaded the book into their data banks.

"Linda, you never cease to amaze me. How did a GPS get so powerful?"

"Beats me, Harry. I just remember a heavyset man with a thick accent named Stanley saying, 'This will be good,' and I was created. I have always been this good, Harry. Now, I am learning there is more to know I am going back into the tent to practice."

"By yourself?"

"Yes, it says so in the book! I told you I am a fast learner."

"What about your solution for Daniel?"

"We will handle that in the morning. Good night, Harry! Turn off the screen please. I have some work to do."

"Good night! Like I said, try not to hurt yourself."

THE DISAPPEARING PASTRAMI SANDWICH

The next morning after Andrew's delightful breakfast, Stephen Childs was picked up by limo and taken to the courthouse. Stephen ran up the courthouse steps, caring a large briefcase and a brown bag protecting a pastrami sandwich.

He pushed his way through the halls, trying to avoid the rush of other attorneys. Aware of a flock of I Can lawyers entering the courtroom, he practiced being as pleasant and reserved as he could. He approached them and gave his best morning speech.

"Good morning, losers! You're very impressive in your matching getups. Did you get a deal at the tall-and-chubby shop?"

I Can's chief counselor, Herman Wale, was not happy to see Stephen. They had butted heads many times in court, with bad results. Wale steadied himself and asked Stephen Childs, "Do you want to settle right now?"

"Sure, Herman, court hasn't started, and we are not on record. Ever since your firm investigated Rudnick and chose him to be the head of development, he's robbed your clients out of tens of millions of dollars. He has been selling your clients' secrets and making promises, with your firm's approval, for fifteen years. Herman, you and your flock are about to get your collective asses kicked today."

"I will bet you that brown-bag lunch against fifty bucks we will shut you down."

"No, Herman. Not even for a thousand dollars would I give up my lunch." Stephen thought for a moment. "Okay, I'll take your fifty bucks."

The court was called to order by Judge Joseph C. Roach, presiding in the case of Mendelbaum v. I Can Corp. "We are setting court hearings and trial dates. Attorney Stephen Childs, representing Mendelbaum, and attorneys Wale, Cohen, Barron, Weiss, Birnbaum, and Pinkie, for I Can, come forward and be heard." Judge Roach focused his attention on Stephen. "Attorney Childs, I am putting you on notice. There will be no yelling in my courtroom today. Do you understand me?"

"Yes, your honor. May I proceed? I am asking for a date for trial in six months."

"Pray tell, since you are suing I Can, why do you want to delay the trial by six months when you could be in court in a month?"

"Because, your Honor, Attorney Wale asked if Mendelbaum would settle this case. Mendelbaum and Levi are bringing litigation against I Can's former employee, Hyman Rudnick. Hyman is currently in a mental hospital police ward. I will be calling all the honorable attorneys, Wale, Cohen, Barron, Weiss, Birnbaum, and Pinkie, as eyewitnesses for the fifteen years of vetting and approving Hyman Rudnick's actions. I will need to take their depositions, and as the court knows, this takes time."

The six attorneys shouted and protested loudly. "We demand a speedy trial!"

"Objections and shouting are overruled. You will appear in my courtroom six months from today! Childs, you were good today, no yelling or cursing. That is why you got what you wanted."

Stephen asked to file the paper for the second trial against Rudnick. Judge Joseph C. Roach smiled and approved the action. Stephen had a good day in court just by behaving himself. With a big smile, he turned to Herman. "That is fifty bucks you owe me, Herman!"

Herman pulled out fifty bucks, grumbling, and gave it to Stephen. He pocketed the bill and handed Herman the brown bag.

"No hard feelings, Herman. Here you go." Stephen walked out of the courtroom. Herman opened the bag and saw that the sandwich was gone. The bag contained nothing but the smell of pastrami, wax paper, used napkins.

"Damn you, Stephen!" Herman tossed the bag on the floor. The judge fined him fifty bucks for littering.

Stephen called Harry with the good news. "Harry, I just got out of court. We filed both lawsuits. I Can's six attorneys folded like a deck of cards!"

"That's good news. Who were the attorneys and what firm?"

"I know them well. The law firm of Wale, Cohen, Barron, Weiss, Birnbaum, and Pinkie. I assure you they won't eat lunch today. Harry, it was beautiful."

LINDA IS MISSING

"Stephen, can you come over? Linda wants to talk to you about some legal matters," Harry said.

"Yes. I can do that. See you soon."

On the screen, Linda was fully dressed, looking like an evangelist's daughter. She was totally covered and wearing a straw hat. "Good afternoon, Harry."

Harry was shocked at her apparel. "Linda, I didn't mean to stop your creativity at dressing the way you did before."

"How do you want me to dress? I thought you were embarrassed by me being stark naked?"

"You have my permission to dress any way you would like. You have been doing great just as you were!"

"So, at night I can run around undressed? It truly is freeing. I like that feeling of freedom." Linda was smiling ear to ear.

"Stephen is on his way to talk to you. Please try not to scare him."

"Shall I let him in just a little? I thought about giving him an earpiece, so he has instant access to me. That would eliminate him having to come over and use your study."

Pausing to consider that idea, Harry said, "Good idea! Please let Stephen know."

Stephen was dropped off at Harry's home. He kissed his hand and touched the *mezuzah*, saying a small prayer. Andrew opened the door and invited him in.

"Thank you. Where am I going?"

"Up to the study to meet with Linda."

Rubbing his belly, Stephen asked, "Is there anything left over from last night?"

"Just some white fish and red onions. Sounds like a snack for you. Would you like a seltzer with that?"

"Just a little snack first and then I will meet with Linda. Do you know what she has up her sleeve?"

Andrew's face glowed red, "I don't know. When I peeked in last time, she was naked with her hair standing straight up. I am not sure if something frightened her or what happened. I haven't been briefed yet."

Stephen thought about that for a moment and said, "Never mind the snack. I will see you later." He ran up the staircase like a young man. He opened the door and peeked in. He saw Linda waiting on the screen. "Where are you this time? Am I ever going to meet you in person?"

"There is something important we need to talk about. Look over on the table by the chair. You will find an earpiece that looks like a tiny hearing aid. Please put it in your ear, and we can talk privately whenever we need to."

"What is this James Bond bullshit? Why can't I see you in person?"

"There are some things better left unsaid for now. We may be able to talk about it later on after the case, but for now, I will be your assistant whenever you need me."

"How much is this going to cost me?"

"Oh, Stephen, don't you understand? I work for Harry. He wants this case to go his way so he can propose to Betty. If he doesn't make this right, Betty might leave him, and he can't stand the thought of that."

"Listen, sweetheart, I have never lost a case. I like the way you make things happen, so we have a deal. But I am still coming over for Langer's. No one does a spread like Harry, and Andrew and I are becoming friends."

Linda sighed. She said that she and the boys would brainstorm new ideas tonight.

He was very pleased, remembering the legal maneuvering in court today.

———

The next day, Stephen's phone rang. It was Harry.

"Stephen, Betty and I want to take you to Spago in Beverly Hills for dinner tonight. Is that good for you?"

"Sure, Harry. They have good *flaggen*. Is Linda coming? I need to meet her and thank her personally. I may even offer her my hand in marriage."

"Linda is busy with the new offices. We'll pick you up at seven thirty to celebrate your great day."

Linda called Stephen after she had listened in on the conversation. "Hello, Stephen. How are you?"

"I was told you're not coming to dinner. Is that true?"

"I can't make it. My crew is working, researching information that will help our cases."

"I could help. I could teach you to dance a tango."

"A sexy dance?"

"Some people think so. Let's go sparking."

Silence lingered when Linda didn't answer him right away.

"Linda, what do you know about sparking?" Stephen was smiling. He knew he got her on this one. "I know quite a few things. I know you can't go with us tonight, but, Linda, be honest. I'm almost forty-five. Am I too old for you?"

"No, you are not too old, Stephen. I have secrets I must be tightlipped about for now. Let's talk tomorrow. Have a good time tonight. Sorry I can't be there."

"Good night. You have my permission to dream about me tonight. Sweet dreams." Stephen took a shower, but his flirting backfired on him, he was aroused and looking for release. Andrew was already rapping on the door.

"Good evening, Stephen. I have a car awaiting your presence."

"Let me get dressed, and I will be right with you."

Andrew waited patiently.

"Okay, Andrew, off to Harry's."

After pulling into Harry's driveway in the new Prius, Stephen watched the group pile in.

"Hello, Betty, Harry, Gloria. It's going to be a friendly night with this tight squeeze. Harry, where's your Bentley?

"The company demanded it back, and with all the exposure we've had lately, we decided to get a more nondescript car."

Andrew, driving, asked the GPS for directions to Spago in Beverly Hills. The GPS voice came on. It was not Linda, but it gave exact directions to Spago.

The restaurant was crowded. The chef came out to meet Harry's party and seat them in the private section.

"Nice place you have here, Waldo," Stephen said.

"Oh, Mr. Childs, it is my pleasure having you here. Harry, how are your parents?"

"Very well, thanks. This is my girlfriend, Betty, her mother, Gloria, and Andrew."

Waldo nodded to each of them. "I'm pleased to see you tonight." He said to his best waiter. "Tony, please take care of my friends."

"I'll do my best."

Tony's best was excellent! Every dish was perfection, including the *flaggen.*

After a full evening and a great meal, everyone was fat and sassy. They were driven home. Harry and Betty adjourned to the master bedroom, leaving Gloria and Andrew alone. They disappeared into the pool house for some private time.

Back at his house, Stephen got ready for bed. He was slipping beneath his sheets when he had an urge to talk one more time to Linda. "Linda, are you here? Hello, Linda?" He adjusted his new earpiece, turned it up, and asked once more. "Hello, Linda, where are you?"

Just then, a chill ran up his back.

"You have reached a disconnected number. Do not ever call back."

His ear started burning, and he pulled the earpiece out. It caught on fire and melted away. He jumped up, grabbed a robe, and rushed to call Harry.

"Harry, I think something happened to Linda!"

"What are you talking about?" Harry leapt out of bed, startling Betty. What's wrong?"

"There is a problem."

"Tell me everything. Stephen, what happened?"

"I was calling Linda, and a man's gruff voice answered, saying, "You have reached a disconnected number. Do not ever call back.' Then my earpiece burned up. What is going on?"

"Get over to my place quickly. We might have a serious problem! Betty, get dressed. Go get Gloria and Andrew from the pool house. Meet me in the study."

Gloria was spending the evening with Andrew. Betty hurried to the pool house to tell her and Andrew to head to the study and ran back to change in Harry's bedroom.

"Did you get them up?"

"Yes, but I won't be able to get that vision out of my head for a long time. I think I am scarred for life! Harry, tell me what's going on."

"It's about Linda. She has disappeared. After Stephen, Gloria, and Andrew get here, I will spill the beans about everything."

Within an hour, a full and tired group gathered in Harry's study. Andrew woke up the staff to supply coffee for everyone. Harry put in his earpiece and tried to call Linda. There was still no answer.

"We have a problem. Linda is missing!"

The lit screen showed Daniel and Ralph, and they saw everyone standing in the study looking at them. Ralph spoke. "Harry! Linda is missing! We can't find her!"

"Hold on. Let me explain how important Linda is. The three of you came into my life on my birthday this year." Harry looked around the study at everyone, including Ralph and Daniel on the screen, looking confused and concerned about Linda. "At my birthday party, everything changed. Betty and I started to date, and I got a huge bonus and lots of gifts. One gift was a new GPS for my car. It was voice operated, and had a beautiful, soothing voice. She started helping me with things other than directions."

There was a buzz in the group when Betty became lightheaded and fell into a chair. "Oh, this may be all my fault. Harry, I'm so sorry."

Harry tried to interrupt Betty, but she stopped him.

"Harry, let me finish. I collected money from employees at the office. I raised one thousand dollars, and I was in charge of buying the gift. I didn't know what you would want for your birthday. I asked a brilliant friend who worked at Starbucks named Stanley Rapouchi what he would recommend—"

"Stanley Rapouchi?" Ralph and Daniel said together.

Daniel continued, "He's applied at every computer company for the last twenty years, and he's been turned down. He is a crackpot."

"I asked him for help. I didn't know what to get a man who had everything. To my best memory, I told him my boss got lost frequently and could not even find elevators. He had been missing appointments, but nobody ever got mad at him for being late because he's such a nice guy. That was when Stanley said he had a quick fix for my problem. He told me he was working on a new project. A supercomputer that took reserve energy from surrounding devices like iPhones, GPS, and laptops. It could make decisions, reason, and build artificial intelligence. He was sure one day it would power robots.

"He had the original prototype that he would sell me. I asked him how much I would have to pay, and he just kept talking, so I listened. He had a job at Starbucks for the next couple of years to accumulate the money he needed to perfect it. He said computer companies thought he was a crackpot. He had a minicomputer that connected to the GPS to make it voice activated. It was supposed to be better than any other GPS, even better than anybody would ever expect. His services are priceless. I told Stanley all I had was one thousand dollars, but he sold it to me, saying he would 'tweak it to perfection.' He told me its name was Linda, and I had it gift-wrapped the next day."

Harry sat down. He started remembering what happened on his birthday. "After I received the gift, I thought I was going crazy. Not only was the GPS talking, but my car started talking back too. Later, on my birthday night, I received the package from Rudnick. It was the prototype I Can cell phone. It also talked, and soon, all three were talking to me and each other. The scary thing was they were all making sense. Yes, I had three new friends. Eventually wanting to be seen, they created their own avatars. That is why you have never seen them in person. Daniel, is there anything you and Ralph can do to help us find her?"

Breaking the silence, Gloria said, "Betty, do you still know that guy, Stanley Rapouchi?"

"I still have his phone number in my contacts!"

Gloria huddled with the big crew and then used Betty's phone to make a call. "Hello, is this Stanley Rapouchi?"

"Yea, this is Stanley. Who's calling?"

"My name is Gloria Levi. I'm the head of Complete Securities Services. I was told you were looking for a job in development. Are you still looking for that position?"

"Why, yes I am. Excuse me a second; I'm checking your credentials." Stanley was silent for a moment. "Gloria Levi, you spent time as the director of security with NATO, and you were the attorney general. I hope you don't mind—"

"Look, Stanley, I have a long-term job opportunity for you. When can we sit down and talk?"

"Now is good for me if it is not too late for you."

"Please give Andrew your address, and he will pick you up."

Within the hour, Stanley was delivered to Harry's home and taken to the study.

Ralph and Daniel appeared on the screen, sitting at a desk and dressed professionally. Harry and Betty were sitting on the sofa. Andrew was guarding the door, and Gloria, loaded for bear, was in charge. Stanley took a seat next to Stephen, and everyone looked at Stanley.

"Stanley, you sold a computer piggybacked on a GPS to Betty, didn't you?" Gloria asked.

"Oh, yes I did. I had been working on that model for years, and I needed money. I sold it to Betty." Stanley looked around the room and spotted Betty. "Oh, hi, Betty."

Stanley tried to get up and move toward the door. Andrew and Gloria pushed him into the leather chair and handcuffed him. They tied his feet together and gagged him with a hankie.

Andrew turned the chair so Stanley could see Gloria washing her hands at the bar sink. Slowly and carefully, she put on rubber gloves, a doctor's mask, and a splatter shield.

"Stanley, we know everything," Gloria said. "Before we do a deep interview with you, we will give you time to tell us what you did with Linda. Are you ready to talk to me?"

Stanley nodded profusely.

"I take that as a yes?"

Andrew removed the gag, pulled up an empty chair, and Gloria sat down on it. She was staring into Stanley's eyes. His face was drenched with sweat. Gloria could smell his fear. The others stood and moved closer around the chair Stanley was lashed to.

"What made you kidnap Linda?"

"I didn't kidnap her. I just recalled her. Betty told me her boss was still using Thomas Brothers maps. I figured he never even learned how to use the GPS, and he wouldn't notice a different voice if he did.

"I am working on a product everybody will need. It's a beautiful stainless-steel and teal-colored electronic device. It connects to Wi-Fi and can be placed on a table in the house. This device can turn on lights, make reservations at restaurants, turn on sprinklers, and call the fire department in case of a fire, even call the police should you be in danger. And, of course, I wanted Linda to be the voice of my newest device. I created her voice to be soothing to the heart."

Gloria smiled at Stanley and put her gloved hand on his thigh, causing him to squirm and sweat.

"Oh my God! You aren't going to kill me, are you? You won't be able to transfer Linda back if you do."

"Are you going to tell me where Linda is?"

"Yes, for God's sake! She is on an eight-hundred-gigabyte stick on my key chain! Okay, I told you! So, you don't need to kill me, right? Think about it, Gloria. I could be of great help to you. I am quite brilliant. I am not a crackpot."

"We were thinking of offering you a job if you cooperated with us. Obviously, you are quite talented. Linda is amazing.

You'll be the director of development at our security company. We'll negotiate a fair salary, but we'll be keeping an eye on you. If you mess up, you know what will happen."

"Okay, Gloria. We have a deal! Untie me and I'll set Linda free."

Daniel and Ralph were jumping up and down. Andrew untied Stanley, took off the handcuffs, and pulled him out of the chair.

Stanley placed his keys and the G800GB stick into Andrew's palm, which Andrew then handed back to Stanley.

"Stick it into the computer, Stanley. Ralph and I will do the rest," Daniel said.

The screen went black, and everyone could hear electronic noise from the backup systems. After minutes of darkness and great anxiety, the screen flashed on and off, and Linda appeared.

"Hi, Harry. I am so happy to see you. I didn't think I would ever be back. Stanley, you're a *schmuck*! I learned that word from Stephen, but I think it describes you to a T."

Music played, and Ralph and Daniel sang background with Linda, who was dressed in a beautiful, black, off-the-shoulder dress. Her hair was done up, and her voice was beautiful. The whole group started singing Joe Cocker's song, "With a Little Help from My Friends."

Linda asked the question everyone was avoiding. "Do we have a fix for Daniel? I have become very attached to him. Stanley, you had me on your key chain for safekeeping. What can you do for Ralph and Daniel to keep all of us safe?"

"If you send me your links, I can copy them and reboot you all back to your original state but updated."

"Harry, it will be your call," Linda said. "I speak for all of us. We never could stand to be separated again."

Linda, Daniel, and Ralph shared a group hug with tears of happiness. *They were having feelings*!

"Stanley, how soon can this be done? Are you sure it'll work?

"Since I'm the director of development, move over and let me use the computer."

Harry opened up his desk, revealing his private computer.

"Damn, Harry, this computer looks like a new Bentley! Linda, can you send me the links now?"

"Already sent!"

His fingers flying across the keyboard, Stanley wrote a program that would keep everything safe and sound. "Everyone ready? Linda, Ralph, Daniel, this will wipe everything clean and bring you back with everything you have learned with no memory loss."

"Please be careful!" Daniel said.

Stanley looked around the room, knowing the seriousness of his task. He looked at the screen and saw all three avatars holding hands and hugging. He pushed the send button, and the screen went blank. "This should take a few minutes. It is uploading a large program."

Five minutes later, it still was still loading. Everyone was getting concerned and looking at Stanley. He was sweating.

"Stanley, what's happening?" Harry asked.

"Please listen up. Great things take time."

A ding. Stanley typed again with fast fingers, and the screen got cloudy. He put the G800GB stick back into the computer, and the screen slowly came into focus. Linda, Ralph, and Daniel were not only back, but they were completely naked!

The screen went dark again, then turned on and the three friends appeared, still holding hands. They stood under a full moon in the desert.

"We are back! We have our full memory. Ralph, Daniel, and I need an hour or two alone to process what we have been through. Thank you for returning us to be with Harry." Linda ran off with Ralph and Daniel into a big tent and closed the flap. The screen then turned off.

"Where are they going, Harry?" Betty asked.

"Catching up on research! Stanley, let me have the stick."

Stanley pulled out the stick, removed his keys, and handed it to Harry.

"Thank you, Stanley. Tomorrow, we start work on our new company. We need your wish list to make us state of the art. We'll partner with you to get our new device into the hands of customers, who will stand in line all day for a device that will not only talk to them but also listen to them and make their lives easier. This will knock I Can out of the game."

Stanley said, If I am going to represent you, I need some cash to move out of my ratty apartment. I need new clothes and a car that runs."

"Look in the closet. I had a wardrobe delivered to the guest-house. It should last you for a week. Tomorrow, we'll get you a company car, an apartment close to our new office, and five hundred dollars in cash. Will that be enough?"

"Damn, Harry, that is more than I was making in two weeks at Starbucks. Thank you. I'm really not a crackpot. I do *sometimes* know what I'm doing."

"You will be reporting to Gloria every day. You can contact Linda and her crew for one hour per week if you need their help."

CLOSING THE DEAL

The trial was set for Harry and Betty versus Hyman Rudnick in three weeks. Attorney Herman Wale showed up to Stephen's office for the case against I Can, offering a settlement.

"Herman, what the hell are you doing here?"

"I came here to make a deal for I Can. We want the one of one back, and we are willing to pay your client for it."

"No, Herman. I want you to know this isn't personal. Your company made a deal with Harry Mendelbaum for three years. Harry kept his word by reporting every six months, even though he could have held out for a year. This is a clear breach of agreement by your company."

"But it is just a phone. What's the big deal? Let's make this simple. My client will pay fifty thousand dollars today. Do we have a deal?"

"Herman, give me a minute, please."

Herman got comfortable in the big chair and nodded.

Stephen left the room and tapped his earpiece. "Linda, are you here?"

"Yes! I heard the deal Herman offered you."

"Are Ralph and Daniel totally out of danger? Is the phone reset to its original settings?"

"Yes, they are all safe. The phone is reset and useless to us. It is a good upgrade, but by 2023, there will be much better phones on the market. I give you Harry's permission to give the one of one back to the I Can company."

"Good news! I will go and make the arrangements and take Herman to lunch."

Stephen went back to his office and saw Herman looking around.

"Stephen, do we have a deal?"

"No, not today. Never for fifty thousand! Herman, I'm going to lunch at Philippe's. You should join me, my treat. I owe you a good lunch."

"I'm not going to court today. I'll go with you, but I'm driving."

They went off to Philippe's on Ord and Alameda. They were lucky and found a parking spot on Ord right in front of the door. They walked down the steps where a busy crowd was standing in lines to get to the counter.

"I love this place. Stephen, we do have something in common. We both like the double-dipped pastrami."

"That's what I like. I'd like to get to the point. What is the real offer? You were bold enough to throw fifty K on the table."

"I was just making an opening offer, hoping I might collect on lunch. I was really pissed off at you for the paper bag trick. Look, I'm not a bad person. We just keep butting heads. Let's make peace, and maybe some pie?"

"Pie! Okay, I'm still buying."

Two hours passed, and they were still at it. Herman's latest offer was five hundred thousand dollars.

"Five hundred grand! Out of the question!"

"How much would a long trial cost your client? I would bet it would cost . . . Hmm, let me think."

In Stephen's ear, Linda summed up what they would charge their clients, including court costs and damages, give or take two percent.

"Okay, Herman. Let's settle this now. Like you said, half a million dollars. How about four hundred fifty grand? That way, you settled and saved your client a shitload of money. You can charge your clients a full day of your time today."

"Stephen, I'm full and want to make a deal. How about rounding it out to three hundred fifty thousand dollars?"

"Nope, four hundred fifty grand is going to be my final answer."

"Okay, let's go back to my office and sign the papers."

Stephen was very pleased with himself.

Herman said, "We'll exchange the phone. I'll write the check and make peace until next time."

Linda heard the conversation and the deal. She made two copies of the legal contracts and sent them to Stephen's printer. When Herman and Stephen walked into the office, Stephen picked up the two sets of documents and handed one set to Herman.

"Damn, you already printed our agreement?" Herman sat down, read the papers, and made no changes. He signed them and wrote the check. He accepted the I Can, without the Tiffany cover, and smiled. "Stephen let's do more lunches. I Can will be pleased with this settlement. I told them we could pay up to five hundred grand."

Linda whispered into Stephen's earpiece, "Great work, counselor."

.

HYMAN BREAKS

The first day at Harry and Gloria's new company went well. What could ever go wrong?

Back at his office, Stephen began work on the Rudnick case. The charges were slander of character, public assault by bullying, slander by proxy, and electronic breach of confidentiality by videotaping and distributing personal videos on every possible public media channel.

Within four weeks, the video had been seen and shared by over two million people. Stephen had been able to disrupt the video sharing for a few weeks, but he discovered that those who'd pulled the video off the internet were now sharing the content again.

"I will ask the court to use Hyman as an example and a warning to all despots and despicable sorts like him."

"Stephen, can I help you?" Linda asked in his earpiece.

"Linda, I think so. I want to go into court fully loaded for a quick win. What I need immediately is an update on Hyman's sanity. Can you do that for me?"

The printer started up.

"Thanks, Linda. Before I read it, does it look like Rudnick can stand trial?"

"He's still in police custody at the hospital. He is doing nicely. Hyman is being medicated on a light dose of barbiturates. He's talking daily with his attorneys.

"The attorneys taped the conversation informing him the one of one was recovered. However, it was useless because it was brought back to the original setting. It was wiped clean of any information except the program he wrote to spy on Harry. And of course the fifty-seven people he sent the video to, including their information."

Linda played the recording:

"What in the hell were you thinking? You will understand this better when we get to court. The judge impounded one of one. It's been taken into custody. Of course, the jury will be viewing the evidence and seeing the video.

"Hyman, you're up to your neck in the big muddy! You have no funds available! The businesses you sold Proprietary *infor-*

mation to are being sued. Your holdings in the company have been revoked. I anticipate all your assets will revert to I Can.

"Sally has taken all your personal property, including the houses. When the divorce is settled, you will get fifty percent of their value. However, we don't know if I Can will attach that as well. As for Sally, your prenup will hold up in court, and she is not fighting it. She is a sweet woman. She is vacationing in Hawaii. I think she deserves it all.

"I want you to understand, Hyman, this is the last time we'll be representing you. Look at me, do you understand what I just said?"

"Yes, Herman. I'm listening. I understand. Thank you for seeing me through the trial!"

"Hyman, as your attorney, my best advice is to plead guilty and throw yourself on the mercy of the court. You're becoming the poster child for hacking, pandering, and bullying. You're looking at a sentence of at least twenty years hanging over your head. I've mentioned this before, but with good behavior and luck, you'll be out of prison within fourteen years."

"Goodbye, Herman. Thanks for the information!"

The sound of someone getting up and walking across the room were heard through the recording before they heard Hyman's voice again.

"Hello! Hello! May I please have my medication?" He started singing a different Hyman song. *"Nobody knows the trouble I've seen. Nobody knows but Jesus."*

The nurse came in with his medication and listened to his pitiful song.

Stephen's mouth hung open.

"Linda! Did you send this to Harry?"

"Yes, I did. For your information, it was attorney Herman Wale who recorded this and sent it to you on a 'For Your Eyes Only' file. Apparently, you made a good friend."

SPARKING

"Linda, can we talk tonight?" Stephen asked.

"Yes! Are you in the mood to go sparking?"

"I don't know how this will work out, but yes!"

That night, Stephen showered, shaved, brushed his teeth, combed his hair, and slapped on his best aftershave, Old Spice. He put on his silk pajamas, had a hot cup of tea, and worked on his Toys for Tots and 3rd Marine Division letters and checks.

He got in bed and began reading a book about traveling in Italy, and as the time went on, he took off his glasses. With tired eyes, he fell into a deep sleep, dreaming about Linda.

He woke up at first light feeling great. He walked into his bathroom and looked into the mirror. What he saw was surprising. He saw sparkling eyes, skin aglow, and an ear-to-ear smile.

The feeling of having the *greatest sex ever* came over him. He found himself singing out loud. His walk now had a spring in each step. He walked back into the bedroom, and his television screen turned on, revealing a smiling Linda.

"Stephen, did you enjoy sparking?" Linda blushed.

"Sure did! I wish I was awake. Is this how it will always be?"

"Yes, Stephen! I want you to know that it was just like a wonderful dream. I care deeply about you as my friend. There are things you need to know. There are only two others like me, Ralph and Daniel. They are my best friends. They are the only ones I actually touch and share feelings with. You do understand that I'm not human, and never will be, right, Stephen?"

"Thanks for last night, Linda. I want you to know you may not be human, but I love you as my counsel and best friend. I think Ralph and Daniel are the luckiest avatars in the world. Do I have your permission to revisit my dreams about you whenever I feel the need to? I'd like to have a real relationship with a nice human girl someday!"

Linda said, "I can help you find a forty-something woman that you would like. Would that be okay?"

"You would help me find that missing piece of my puzzle?"

"I will, but now, we need to stay focused on work."

Stephen knew that the Rudnick case would be difficult, even with all the evidence he had. "You know, in court anything can happen. Linda, how much paperwork do we have on the case?"

"About three hundred and fifty pages. Shall I print them for you in order of priority, as well as the subpoena papers to file with the court?"

"Yes, that would be very helpful. I need to call Herman to arrange a suitable date for all concerned."

"Would you like me to call Herman to set the court dates, including his depositions and those of the rest of the firm of Cohen, Barron, Weiss, Birnbaum, and Pinkie?"

Stephen was amazed at Linda's immediate efficiency. "Yes, we can do the depositions here in our offices in a peaceful manner and even provide lunch and cookies."

"I wouldn't expect anything less from you, Stephen. On the bright side, I have arranged a date for you on Saturday night with a nice woman who would like to go out for a playdate with you. She is an attorney about your age."

"Who is she? Do I know her?"

"Yes, you do know her. Her name is Margaret Farmer."

"Margaret Farmer would go out with me? She is a knockout. Are you sure she knows it's me?"

Linda laughed. "Yes, I talked to her about you. She said you two met in college, and she thought you were cute and so intelligent. She'd love to go out with you."

"Linda, this might be better than Langer's pastrami!"

"Stephen, have you gone out on a lot of dates in the last few years?"

"Yes, I get out a lot."

"I will take that as a no! Stephen, it is 2018, and things have changed since you were in college. I'm going to ask you some personal questions. Is that okay with you?"

"Yes, you may ask me anything."

"Stephen, you already have your contracts and a health card, right?"

"What the hell are you talking about?"

"It is now customary and prudent on a first date to have mutual consent forms before having sex, as well as a card from your doctor stating you are currently free of any STDs, like Syphilis or HIV, or any other diseases."

Stephen sat back in his chair and dropped his pen on his desk. He shook his head, opened a Coke, and downed it. "Linda, are things always on the table starting with a first date?"

"That's a big ten four! Stephen, everyone is playing poker with their cards facing up. Go out and have some fun. A new dream just might come true."

YOU HAVEN'T HEARD THE LAST OF ME

The next week Harry, Stephen, Gloria, and Andrew were busy working with the crew to get ready for the upcoming court date. They were making sure everything was in order.

Stephen was staring at the blackboard, pointing at the timeline. "This looks like fifteen days in court. We only have ten days to make it work."

Daniel and Ralph asked, "Is Rudnick going to be able to appear in court or might he plead insanity?"

Stephen asked Linda, "What would we do in case he does?"

Linda researched what their options would be. "Stephen, we can request our own doctors examine him. Other than that, the chips will fall where they may."

"Linda, we could, but you know me! I don't give up that easy. That schmuck pisses me off! He was just fine before he got arrested. Why, now, is he crazy? We can't call Sally Rudnick as a witness because wives can't testify against their husbands and Hyman knows that. She was our friend in high school. Harry dated her for three years. All I know is that something happened in a pool house, and she broke up with him.

"She never really cared about Hyman. He offered her a cushy life with everything she wanted. She needed to get away from her parents, so Sally took it. Besides, Gloria told me she was serving her freshly baked cookies during his arrest. I don't think she was actually heartbroken when they took him away."

"Stephen, you are so bad!" Linda said. "Will this affect Harry and Betty if Sally testifies? Is there anything she could say that would make Harry look bad?"

"Linda, this is client/attorney privilege. I am sworn to secrecy, not only as Harry's attorney, but as his friend."

"That doesn't mean Sally is sworn to secrecy."

"Trust me! Linda, there is nothing Sally will want to talk about, and it has nothing to do with Rudnick."

The wheels started turning at the office; the case was on its way. They knew Rudnick could not pull off his insanity plea and things were going to get hot.

***Hyman Rudnick was very busy in the hospital ward of the prison. He had been transferred from San Francisco two weeks ago. He was in federal custody. For the last ten days, he had been pocketing his meds. He knew he needed to have a clear and focused mind for court.

Hyman had a plan. He requested his attorneys give him the arguments they would be using, law books, the use of a laptop computer, and a small screwdriver. To his amazement, he got everything he had asked for.

Hyman went to work. After all, he was the best hacker in the country. He was incarcerated with very little supervision.

Hyman started his plan. First, he ordered a full wardrobe for court and traveling, including a large suitcase.

He hacked into the court's mainframe and ordered his own release for that very night after nine p.m. for "no cause to hold and without bail."

He rescheduled his court date six months forward. His wallet, credit cards, and a few thousand in cash were to be the first items returned. Next to arrive was a large package of new clothing from Neiman Marcus. Neiman's had, on file, all of his sizes, from hat to shoes with everything in between.

That evening, Hyman dressed and was ready. He had eight days of new clothing in his new luggage. He created a new identity and credit cards with unlimited credit delivered to him at the front desk of the Bonaventure Hotel.

A nurse and guard arrived exactly at nine p.m. with his release orders. They handed them to Hyman and checked his arm tags, then cut them from his wrist.

The nurse said, "Hyman, remember to take your pills and see your doctor as soon as possible. Hyman, do you have someone picking you up? You are not allowed to drive until you are off your meds."

"Yes, I do, thanks! I'm glad to be going home. Thanks for sitting and singing with me when I really needed some company."

The guard was not impressed. "Let's go! It's getting late, and I'm missing *Game of Thrones*."

THE BONAVENTURE HOTEL

Hyman was taken to the prison's discharge window where he was given back his personal items. He was escorted to the door on Hill Street, pulling two pieces of luggage to an awaiting limousine he ordered at the same time he ordered the clothing.

The driver put his luggage in the trunk and held the door open. Hyman turned and handed the nurse five hundred dollars.

"Sir, my name is Tim," the driver said. "Where would you like to go?"

"The Bonaventure. Tim, is this your limo?"

"Yes, sir!" He stood taller. "It's my business. I have three cars. My wife and brother-in-law drive the others."

"Excellent, can you be my driver for a month?"

"Sir, my daily rate is seven hundred dollars!"

"Okay, Tim. While we are traveling, I will pay for your food, hotels, and expenses. Here's an advance of two thousand dollars. On second thought, what kind of car does your wife drive?"

"A Lincoln Town Car."

Hyman replied, "I'll take that also. Does she mind traveling?"

"Not when we are being paid!"

"You will have a suite starting tonight. Tell her to pack a month's worth of clothing for you both. We'll be here, in Los Angeles, only for the weekend!"

At the Bonaventure, Tim opened Hyman's door and the trunk. He began getting the luggage out when Hyman stopped him.

"Tim! Please let the attendants load and unload the car from now on."

"Yes, sir." Then with authority to the attendant, he said, "Please unload the luggage!"

The attendant jumped up, quickly unloaded and racked Hyman's cases, and brought them to the front desk.

"I have a reservation," Hyman said.

The attractive woman at the desk smiled and welcomed Hyman by his fictious name. "Mr. Grover, we were expecting you. Here is your package. It was delivered for you today."

Hyman—now Mr. Karl Grover—smiled, opened the package, and pulled out his new ID card. He handed it to the beautiful, thirty-something hotel manager, whose name tag read: Ms. Prudence Cline.

"Karl, everything is in order. Because you're using your American Express Centurion Card, all your bar tabs will be complimentary!"

"Why thank you, Prudence. Please put my driver up on my floor. Make sure my cars are parked in the driveway, not in the garage. We'll be staying through Monday morning. And I have one last request. Will you have dinner with me in my room tonight?"

Prudence whispered, "Karl, I would be happy to have dinner with you. I get off work at eleven o'clock. Is that okay for you?"

"Yes, I even have my health card with me."

"Your what?"

"I haven't dated for a while. My friend said that was what was required these days?"

Prudence handed a key card to Tim. "Everything is comped for your stay."

Tim felt like he was dreaming. "My wife will be coming tonight. Please have a key for her, and please park her car in the driveway next to mine."

"Of course. Shall I order a special midnight dinner for your room?" Tim looked at Karl, who nodded. "Yes, please."

"Done! Thank you for staying at the Bonaventure!"

That evening, at 11:05 p.m., Prudence came to Karl's door with a procession of waiters and dinner for two, including a couple of bottles of wine and two bottles of chilled Dom Pérignon champagne.

"Prudence, you're not a minute late."

She immediately instructed the waiters to set dinner on the table. With a nod of her head, they left them alone.

Karl smiled. "What comes first?"

She uncorked the Veuve Clicquot Ponsardin and champagne. She filled two glasses and handed one to Karl. She picked up her glass and spilled it down the front of her blouse. "Whoops, now what am I supposed to do?" She removed her blouse. "Karl, let's have a drink, have some food, and find out what makes each other scream!"

"Scream?"

On the table was a large, covered dish. Prudence walked up to Karl and pulled off his shirt. She reached over to the covered dish and unveiled a nasty-looking, two-foot whip!

She quickly pulled off the rest of her clothes, revealing a cut-out, tight, leather dominatrix outfit. Karl's eyes were like saucers, and fear made him freeze.

For the rest of the night in the suite next door, Tim and his wife heard the crack of a whip and Karl yelling, "Yes! I'm a bad boy! Yes! I'm a bad boy!"

At one point, Mistress Prudence stepped on Karl's feet and said, "Beg for it, you nasty little shit!"

"Please send me the video! I need the video! I'm a very bad boy!"

"I will be posting it for my best friends!" Prudence was laughing a nasty laugh.

"Anything you want. Do it again! I am a very bad boy!"

"All right, Karl. I will send a copy to you, so you won't forget me."

The next day, the video was posted on Prudence's site and her social media pages. In the morning when Karl awoke up from an exhausting evening, he was sore in places he didn't know he had. For the rest of the weekend, Karl didn't leave his suite.

———

On Monday morning, Tim and his wife, Samantha, instructed the parking attendants to load the luggage while they stood by and supervised. Karl was checking out at the front desk.

Ms. Prudence said, "Good morning, Karl. How was your stay?"

"To tell you the truth, Ms. Prudence, it was a bit more than I expected."

"Will you be returning soon?"

"When I recover in a few months."

"Karl, I'm sure there will be a next time. I'll make a note in your file. Have a nice day." Prudence winked and smiled at Karl.

He shivered and smiled back. Karl limped to the exit and into the limousine. "Tim, here is a list of three friends who will be going to San Francisco with me. Send the Town Car to pick them up."

With knowing smiles, Tim and Samantha waved at each other and were off to San Francisco. There were a lot of stories in the big city.

The video Ms. Prudence had posted had been edited. Only her body was shown, except one scene with a shot of her blurred face. Karl, a.k.a. Hyman Rudnick, was in full view! The video that was being "liked" on Prudence's website started being shared by her followers.

Hyman slept and dreamed "I'm a very bad boy" over and over again, speaking loud enough for Tim to hear. He was laughing to himself that he was getting paid to be in an extravagant circus. He said out loud, "You just can't make this shit up!"

GAMES PEOPLE PLAY

Stephen's first date with Margaret Farmer went better than he'd expected. The day began at a cozy restaurant in the Beverly Center, a shopping extravaganza in Los Angeles, and ended up in the front seat of Stephen's new black-on-black GT500 Mustang.

Driving to Santa Monica, the two lawyers discovered they had quite a few things in common.

"Stephen, you're very nice! I like you, and I would like to know you better."

Stephen drove onto the Santa Monica Pier. "Margaret, let's play and have some fun at Nickel Heaven." For the next three hours, they played every game at the arcade from Skee-Ball to Whack-a-Mole. They were laughing, holding hands, and winning tons of tickets from each game.

Stephen whispered to Margaret that he would like to get a hotel room at the beach and have some fun. They found a boutique hotel and checked into the best suite they had.

"Stephen! This is a big room!"

"Better to run around in. Margaret, let's get this playdate started." Stephen was excited as he watched Margaret hurry to the small dining room table.

She opened her suitcase, pulled out a green felt cloth, and covered the table. Not to be outdone, Stephen opened his suitcase and whipped out five decks of cards, a game of UNO, dominos, and Yahtzee. "Game on. Playdate!"

Margaret played a mean game of canasta. Stephen excelled playing Yahtzee. They counted their winnings to see who won the right to make the first move.

Margaret kicked it up a notch by suggesting they go to the bedroom and play hide-and-seek. This is when things got serious. She ran into the bedroom, changed her clothes, and got under the covers.

Stephen ran into the closet and came out dressed like a cowboy looking for his cattle. "Come out, come out. Olly Olly oxen free." Stephen quietly grabbed the covers, and in one hard pull, off they came!

She stood on the bed, in all her glory, in a shorty nightgown and wearing a Godzilla head mask.

Stephen yelled, "Yahoo!"

Margaret roared and pretended to blow fire. The playdate was on. Not just sex, but a wonderful friendship was happening! Within an hour, the room looked like a war zone—clothes all over and games on the floor.

Stephen and Margaret were exhausted, lying on the bed with their arms wrapped tightly around each other. They were sleeping with smiles on their faces, both dreaming of what would come next.

The sun came through the window, waking Stephen and Margaret. She kissed him on the lips. "Stephen, you are the first person I ever played Godzilla with! Sorry about your shirt."

Stephen said, "Don't worry about that. Can I ask you a personal question?"

"Yes, you can."

"You make me feel like singing. Does that bother you?" Stephen sang:

"They say falling in love is wonderful. Wonderful, now that I've found you."

"The feelings are mutual. May I make a stipulation that we need more bedtime to work this out? What do you say, counselor?"

"I say, yahoo!"

Stephen and Margaret canceled their workday. About to pull the earpiece out of his ear, Stephen heard Linda whisper, "Good work, my friend. Aren't human girls more fun? Now, you have a smart one of your very own. Have fun! By the way, she really is beautiful. See you tomorrow at the office."

Stephen felt so lucky. He turned to find Margaret in the bedroom. She was wearing a Robin Hood costume, including a bow and arrow. This woman was the one.

I CAN STRIKES BACK

Gloria and Andrew had a new powerful client, so they were working late. The client had top-secret clearance that took him away from home quite a bit.

He was fearful his wife was seeing another man, which would compromise his identity. Andrew felt he needed more information. He had a bad feeling about this man, and his intuition was telling him something wasn't right. "Mr. Swain, what makes you think your wife's having an affair?"

"She covers her cell phone, or she will close it down when I walk in the room. Sometimes I can't reach her by cell. She's been telling me she forgot to charge her phone."

Gloria asked, "Does she have a job?'

"Yes. She has a little job. It is just to have something to do. I'm the breadwinner in our family."

Andrew was feeling impatient and leaned forward in his chair. "Mr. Swain, what do you want us to do? We offer top surveillance, but this is not our usual case."

My Swain was getting red-faced. "I need to know if I'm right and who this man is. My career depends on it."

Gloria looked at Andrew, then at Mr. Swain. "Are you all right? You seem to be sweating. Excuse us for a few minutes so Andrew and I can discuss your case and see what we can offer you."

Andrew and Gloria went into the office, and Andrew said, "We are not taking this case!"

Gloria argued back. "Yes, we are! His security is breeched. We have all the newest equipment to help this man."

Andrew, angry with Gloria for the first time since they met, said, "No, I won't do it."

While they were arguing, their desktop computer lit up. Linda, Ralph, and Daniel appeared on the screen, shushing them and holding up a note. They sent a text to both of them that read: "Don't talk!"

The next text read: "That was a setup just to get into our offices. He just set a bug under the chair he was sitting on, and he dropped another one in the plant by the door."

Andrew walked back into the conference room. "Mr. Swain, I empathize with your situation, but this is not really the kind of case we take on." He saw him to the door, where the overhead cameras were filming him. Andrew came back into the office to talk to Linda.

"Andrew, retrieve the bugs, place them in an empty jar, and cover it tightly," Linda said.

Andrew went to the coffee machine to get an instant coffee jar. He retrieved the two bugs and placed them safely in the jar.

Linda said, "It won't take long to see who is trying to bug us. Let's get Stanley in here to help us crack this."

Andrew called Stanley, and half an hour later, he strolled into the office. "So, what do we have?"

Andrew handed him the jar. After a close look, Stanley pulled out a pocket scanner and looked closely.

"What we have here is a very expensive bug made by I Can. We need to scan the building for more."

"Ralph and Daniel are on it right now!" Linda said.

Gloria took Andrew by the arm and whispered, "I'm sorry." Back to her assertive self, she said, "This smells like Hyman Rudnick. I'm going to call James at the FBI."

It wasn't long before Gloria had her friend on the phone. "James, have you got a minute?"

"Yes, Gloria, I was just going to call you. I have some bad news. Hyman got his hands on a computer. He hacked the courthouse system on Friday night. He got himself released! We have all agencies on this with *all-points alerts* in every state. He has a seventy-two-hour head start."

"I'll alert my crew to help. We just had a client leave a few electronic bugs here. We are working on it. We don't know who did this, but we do know he came from I Can."

"Thanks, Gloria, we're on it. You might not want to see this it is very sexually graphic. of Hyman and a woman, but with facial recognition, we are on Hyman's trail. Friday night, he started appearing all over public media."

"James, who's helping him?"

"We just found out who the creep was who showed up at your office is. We recognized him from your office tapes. Our facial recognition identified him as George Binsky. He worked with Hyman at I Can. It looks like Hyman is putting together a hacking crew. Back to the video of Hyman . . . It is possible to recognize the woman, even though her face blurred. We will work on it and get back to you."

"Linda?" Gloria asked when she disconnected her call.

"Yes, Gloria."

"Will you send me a copy of that video?"

"Gloria, it's not a Disney video."

What do mean?"

"It is painful to watch."

Gloria looked at Linda and said, "It can't be any more painful for me than seeing my daughter's."

Linda agreed. "Okay, Gloria. Have a look at your cell screen."

"Oh my God!" Gloria watched Hyman get whipped as he repeated, "I'm a bad boy."

"What the hell? Dammit, hit him harder. That bastard."

Andrew walked in and saw the look on Gloria's face. He asked what was going on, and she showed him the video. His face turned bright red. "Gloria, what are you watching?"

"It's Hyman!"

"Hyman! How did this happen?"

"He just got away a day or so ago. Listen, Andrew! Hyman is capable of anything. He has people who are helping him. We need to stay on our toes. When you saw the video, I couldn't tell if you were embarrassed or if there is something you are hiding from me and not telling me."

"Well! I . . . I guess I have to admit . . . I tried that a time or two."

Gloria lifted an eyebrow. "We will talk about that later. Right now, we have work to do."

Still red-faced, Andrew said, "Yes, ma'am!"

———

Stephen told Margaret it was time to get back to the office to work on a big case. "Do you want to come with me and meet my partners?"

"No, Stephen, I'm tired and need to get home and rest up for our next date."

Stephen showered and sang in Yiddish. He was never so happy. He got into the car and called Linda, wanting to tell her all the details.

Linda said, "We have some serious things to talk about. Get your *tushy* into the office. We need you."

"Can you give me a hint?"

"Stephen, just get yourself here."

Stephen pulled into the driveway of his office and ran into the building. "What's going on around here? I have only been gone one day!"

Linda appeared on his computer screen. "Hyman got himself a computer. He was able to get himself out of jail, and he's gone. We don't know where he is. You need to do something with the courts to turn this around. He created release papers with no bail. A video showed up today. Do you want to see it?"

"*Oy vey!* Am I in it?"

"No, Stephen! It is Hyman and a dominatrix. It was filmed Friday night."

"*Oy*, another damn video. When can I see it?"

"It's already on your phone. Watch it, and tell me what you see."

Stephen watched the video and said, "Oh, boy. I know her. Linda, I stayed at the Bonaventure one night when court went late and I had to appear early the next morning. She's the front desk woman and manager for the hotel's special clients. We got to talking, and she came up to my room at eleven p.m. That's when she got off work."

Linda raised her eyebrows; she was surprised. "Stephen, I had no idea."

Stephen got a little red-faced. "What do you mean? All she asked was if I could represent her in a case against a man who used her off-hours services and gave her a bad cashier's check." He smiled, knowing he had a good answer, and thanking God silently; he didn't want to look like a *schmuck* to Linda.

"Oh, Stephen, you are amazing. Let's call James and give him this information."

"Oh, she is a nice *shiksa*. I don't want to get her into trouble."

"Stephen, really? It's Harry and Betty we're protecting, remember?"

"Oh, yeah. When you put it that way, of course, make the call."

———

Linda appeared on Gloria's screen and gave her all the details so she could call James.

Gloria was weary. "You know Betty has made our life pretty crazy by getting involved with Harry, but I wouldn't trade it for anything."

"Yes, if it weren't for Betty, I wouldn't be here either," Linda said. "I would never have met Daniel and Ralph or the rest of you. That Betty is a keeper."

Gloria called James, and he issued a warrant for the arrest for Prudence for prostitution and aiding a fugitive.

Stephen Making Miracles

Stephen called Herman and invited him to lunch. "Herman, we have things to talk about. Meet me at Langer's, so at least we can enjoy part of this day."

They met. Stephen ordered his usual number nineteen, a pastrami sandwich, and Herman surprised him by ordering a salad.

"What kind of nonsense is that?" Stephen asked. "You ordered a salad?"

"My doctor said no more pastrami. My cholesterol's through the roof."

"Oh, what does that *schmuck* know? Jews have eaten pastrami for hundreds of years. Okay, be a pussy. We need to talk. Hyman hacked into a computer and got himself released from prison, and no one knows where he is. You need to help us find him and get him back here to stand trial."

"I like you, Stephen, but why should I help you?"

Stephen reached into his pocket, pulled out a small, sealed bottle, and handed it to Herman. "This is why. We had an interview with a client, and when he left, our security found five electronic devices, all made by I Can. Look at these photos our security cameras captured."

"Stephen, we're not bugging you! That is an employee, George Binsky. We fired him over two years ago. He was working with Hyman Rudnick."

"That's exactly what the FBI said. Herman, I know it's not your company that bugged us. Hyman is the culprit. He's using your equipment and your former employee to start a hacking network. We need to stop this before it causes damage to both of our interests."

Herman called the server over. "Can you please change my order to a large plate of pastrami and fries?" He turned to look at Stephen. "Stephen, we'll help you. What do you want?"

"A list of any employees who worked with Rudnick for the last five years to turn over to the FBI!"

"We can do that. You will have it this afternoon."

———

Back at the office, Stephen picked up the phone and called Margaret.

"Hello, Stephen, are we still on for tonight?"

"Of course! I'm looking forward to seeing you and having fun. I have some new games to play!"

"Sounds like a fun night."

"Margaret, I have a client for you if you'll accommodate her. Her name is Ms. Prudence Cline, a dominatrix working out of the Bonaventure Hotel. She was arrested this morning. I can't help her because she is a witness for our firm against Hyman Rudnick."

"Gee, that sounds like it might hurt. Okay, I'm going to court. I need to be there by three o'clock. Is she still incarcerated?"

"Yep. I'll call the feds and list you as her attorney. I gotta go now, kisses and a hug!"

"Back at you! See you tonight."

Betty and Harry walked into Stephen's office. "How did your meeting go today?"

"I met with Herman, and the way he is eating Tums, we should buy stock in the company. He's sending a list of the people who worked with Hyman. I'll forward it to Gloria to give to the FBI."

Harry asked Stephen, "Do you think we will find him? He has the means to disappear anywhere in the world."

"That bastard can't get away with all the damage he has done to so many people, including you and Betty. We want to catch him and make him pay."

Harry was weary. "I'm already tired, and going through a long trial seems pretty daunting to me. I can only imagine what it will do to Betty. We would really like to go on with our lives and have this all go away."

"Harry, I'm your friend and your attorney, and I'll be there for you. Betty and our team of Linda, Daniel, Ralph, Gloria, and Andrew can't be stopped. That Linda is a prize! She has paperwork printing on my printer before I even finish my sentence. You're one lucky *mench*, my friend, having Linda in your life . . . and a human woman too.

———

Attorney Margaret Farmer finished up in court. She was on her way to the holding cell of her new client. She passed security, went into the county lockup, presented papers, and was escorted in.

"Prudence Cline? I'm your attorney. My name is Margaret Farmer. I'm here to make sure you are represented when you go to court."

"Thank you, Margaret. I think I'm in big trouble. I lost my job on Sunday because of the video."

"What video?"

"The video I took of Karl Grover. He's a rich guy. My night job is a dominatrix, working out of my suite at the Bonaventure Hotel. My day job is concierge for VIPs checking into the hotel. I greet them at the front desk and take care of *all* their needs. Don't get me wrong; I'm not a hooker. I just sell the videos to my private clients for cash."

"Did you know that Karl Grover was really Hyman Rudnick?"

"No, I didn't. He had proper ID and lots of unlimited credit on his AMEX card. He invited me to dinner in his suite. I agreed."

"And then what happened?"

"I'm very good at my night job. We made a video! You can see it on the web www.ms.prudence.spanking.the@monkey.com. I have private clientele who pay me twenty-five hundred dollars per month for the privilege of watching my performance art."

"I need to see what is on the video."

"Sure, the code is 2269forU."

Margaret punched in the code and watched the video. "Damn, that must leave a mark! How many clients do you have paying for this service?"

"About five hundred and sixty or so."

"Do you ever charge the customers?"

"Never, ever! That would be hooking, and I'm not a prostitute! I just fill their mommy-wound fantasies, and they allow me to use their videos."

"Prudence. I will get the charges dropped if you will provide a deposition about the time you spent with Hyman. There might be a possibility you could get your job back. Are you willing to proceed?"

"Yes! You bet your sweet ass! I would like to make this go away."

"My last question for today is between us. Am I making myself clear?

"Yes, it's as clear as the smile on your face."

"Where did you get that leather ensemble?"

"I made it myself. I was a seamstress in a leather factory for a few years. I can make you an exact copy if you would like, or I have a new one you could use, then I'll make you your own wardrobe."

"I'd like to wear it with my new partner."

"Margaret, with your hot body, you'd be crazy not to."

"I'll arrange bail for you first thing in the morning. I'll bring you to my office for your deposition. Then, I'll present a writ to the judge tomorrow afternoon."

"Sounds great to me. What will this cost me?"

"Remember, you get what you pay for."

"I'm not worried. My video company makes over 100K each month!"

"Do you give lessons to neophytes?"

"No, but for helping me, I will teach you the basics. That's all you really need."

Both women laughed and shook hands.

PRUDENCE'S DEPOSITION

James received the names from Herman at I Can. He sent the list to Gloria, and she shared it with Linda and the crew. It took a few hours to find the location Hyman and his three friends had traveled to only twenty-four hours ago.

Linda was briefing Gloria about the details. "They were driven to San Francisco, where Rudnick and three dismissed I Can employees changed identifications. They purchased over fifty thousand dollars of electronics, tools, and a large number of screwdrivers. They had enough tools to start up a serious hacking operation. An internet company was hacked, and their bank accounts emptied. A large amount of gold, used for jewelry manufacturing, was purchased from a refinery for fifteen million in cash."

"What about photos of all four?"

"We have all the photos. The FBI has been searching major cities along the West Coast with facial recognition equipment. We had a hit in Seattle, Washington, but it's cold. A private jet with excessive equipment was noted, but no flights took off twenty hours ago. Hyman and crew could be anywhere now.

"We will ask the Federal Aviation Administration to check flights from Washington State for the last twenty hours. We at least will have a direction to look for them. They are most likely heading to a country they can sell their services to, possibly Russia." Gloria brought the whole crew into the office.

Linda, Ralph, and Daniel were on the screen. Andrew was standing next to Gloria, Harry, and Betty. Stephen and Stanley were standing by.

Gloria spoke to everyone present. "We must bring Hyman and his crew to justice, not only for Harry and Betty but for the damage they could cause. I asked Linda to turn over all our files to James at the FBI, including the deposition I am taking tomorrow morning of Prudence Cline. We are pulling strings to have the court free her for her cooperation. We have finally cleared the airways of the video of Harry and Betty that Hyman released. We will still monitor every day until it is nothing but a memory." She paused and slowly looked around the room at each person. "I have one more announcement. Andrew just proposed to me, and I accepted."

A collective cheer went up from the security team.

The next morning, Attorney Margaret Farmer brought Ms. Prudence Cline in for a deposition. She produced the video that was released by her client and was now going viral on the internet. Margaret deposed her for three hours and acquired all the information she needed.

Toward the end, she told Prudence she would make sure the charges were dropped against her if she was a cooperative witness in finding Hyman.

Prudence thought about it for a second. "My client list is filled with very high-profile men. They come to me because they know I will keep every name confidential. I've never released a name of a client, ever. Now you're asking me to do that! It would ruin my business."

At that moment, they heard a commotion outside the door. James and his team had arrived. He told the crew that the Russian government had been informed that Hyman might be in their country. The Russian police had intercepted Hyman and his crew at the airport. They'd confiscated all their equipment, gold, cash, and an airplane.

Attorney Farmer looked at Prudence and said, "Well, I guess that takes care of the case against you at the moment. You'll still be released. However, if Hyman is ever returned to the United States, they will most likely reopen the case. They can't arrest you for what you do for a living since you don't have sexual relations with the men you see. You provide a different kind of service that's not illegal. Let's go celebrate with the team."

Everyone on the team voted to celebrate in style.

Harry asked the crew, "Everyone agree?"

A unanimous "Yes sir!" resounded through the room.

"Of course," Stephen said. "Let's go to Langer's!"

Harry said, "Stephen, you don't get to pick."

"We're going to the Pacific Dining Car, where we can have our own private room. We've got a double celebration! Hyman's capture and Andrew and Gloria's wedding announcement."

Linda asked, "Can you bring us on your iPad? Gloria, I would love to plan your wedding. I can arrange everything, and you wouldn't have to be bothered with it."

Gloria smiled. "I heard you three were amazing planners. I'm sure I would be in great hands. How do I arrange to bring you to find my wedding dress?"

"I can be transferred to your phone for the day, and we'll go shopping."

"A great idea."

When they arrived at the Pacific Dining Car, the seating arrangements were Harry and Betty, Gloria and Andrew, Stephen and Margaret, James and Prudence, and the three members of the FBI support group. Harry held his iPad up and Linda, Daniel, and Ralph were there on the screen sitting at their own table having dinner.

A man at the bar yelled out, "Oh my God! I can't believe what I am seeing! The evening news is on, and they are showing a man wanted for espionage getting spanked and yelling, "I am a very bad boy."

Harry heard him, and they all ran to the bar to watch Hyman in his full glory. "Revenge is sweet."

Linda said, "No. Living well is the best revenge. We never let him break us up. You and Betty stood together against him. We are a great team."

Prudence turned to Margaret. "Are you sure you want me to be here? I don't want to embarrass you."

"Prudence, you're a successful businesswoman. You were released. Yes, of course you can be here as my guest. Besides, I'm waiting for some outfits I can wear for Stephen."

"I don't know about Stephen. He would rather eat than have sex. I never saw a man turned on by a pastrami sandwich or giving toys to children who would have no presents at Christmas before."

"Oh, Prudence, there is another side of Stephen you don't know. He's actually a wonderful lover. He just never found the right woman before me. Besides, I don't want to hit him. I just want to wear the outfits."

The dinner went on, drinks were served, and everyone was getting very friendly, especially James and Prudence.

After a few drinks, James asked, "Prudence, tell me, what is your outfit

de jour?"

"I happen to have a menu. Want to see it?"

James grinned. "Guess not. I can't end up on a bar's television screen. I was just curious." However, they were holding hands under the table where no one could see.

The ride home was quite funny. Stephen told jokes; they laughed so hard their stomachs hurt. After dropping everyone off, Harry, Betty, Andrew, and Gloria were back at Harry's home, tired and happy.

Harry and Betty crawled into bed. Harry held Betty in his arms. "Betty, as much as we have been through, you have to admit, life is pretty damn good. How about we have a playdate?"

"Give it up, Harry! I'm tired. Can we just snuggle?"

"Are we really at this place in our relationship already?"

"Oh, Harry, give it up and go to sleep."

In the guest house, Gloria and Andrew were quite a different story. Gloria took off her clothing to reveal a skintight black leather outfit. Andrew wore a smile that lit up the room. There'd be no sleeping in their room tonight!

The four met in the dining room for breakfast the next morning. Harry was grumpy, and Andrew was beaming. Betty and Gloria were discussing the upcoming wedding. They finished breakfast and went to talk to Linda about the plans.

"What are you so damn happy about this morning?" Harry asked once the women had left.

"That Gloria is a knockout! I can't thank you enough for introducing me. She has the energy of a teenager."

Harry grumbled, "See you at the office."

In Harry's office, Betty and Gloria were sitting in front of the TV talking to Linda, who appeared on the screen. She was sitting at a table with bridal magazines scattered in front of her. Idea after idea regarding wedding dresses, flowers, invitations, centerpieces, and decorations were everywhere. It was dizzying to Gloria, and she finally said, "Let's stop for now. I forgot how many details needed to be decided on, and I'm already exhausted."

Betty looked at her mom with a curious look on her face. "Why are you so tired? You're a morning person."

"Andrew and I were up all night."

"Why? Did you have a fight?"

"Fight? Are you serious? I wore my outfit that Prudence gave me."

"Mom! TMI! Give it a rest. I was traumatized by walking in on you two. I don't want to hear any details."

"Okay, honey."

WEDDING PLANS

Gloria and Harry met with new clients, the owners of a software company in Century City. Alex and John, partners since they were in their early twenties, came upon a way to connect video gaming and dating. They were very concerned about being hacked and wanted top-of-the-line security for their clients.

Harry and Gloria knew all about hacking,

Harry had told them, "Entrust your clients in my hands. I won't disappoint you." Harry used his charm and sealed the deal. It felt like his old days at Malexion.

Harry turned to Gloria. "How about a celebration dinner tonight?"

"Not tonight, Harry. Linda, Betty, and I are going to pick out my wedding dress."

An hour later, Betty, Gloria, and Linda were off to find the perfect wedding dress. Linda directed them down Melrose Avenue to Betsey Johnson's, where they were holding a dress Linda found online.

Gloria said, "Remember, Linda, a second-wedding dress is not all lacy and fancy. I need something low-key and tasteful."

They walked into the shop and were stunned by the wild outfits. Gloria, wide-eyed, took the phone and looked at Linda.

Linda said, "Relax, Gloria, trust me."

The saleswoman came out to greet them, and Betty introduced her mother.

Marcia said, "Oh, Gloria, we have the perfect dress for you waiting in the dressing room."

Gloria entered the small dressing room to find the perfect, cream-colored suit. She tried it on, and it fit like a glove.

"Gloria, you will be a stunning bride," Marcia said.

"I don't know how you accomplish what you do, Linda, but I am ever so grateful. It's has been a great day. Let's go home."

———

The next morning, Harry was driving to the office. He tapped his earpiece button to get Linda's attention.

"Hi, Harry. Things are going quite well. Don't you think? Is there anything I can do for you?"

"Linda, I miss being on the road, seeing my doctor friends, taking them to lunch, and setting up those dinner meetings. Since you, Ralph, and Daniel came into my life, it has become quite exciting. I had a great life, but exciting it wasn't. I never did exciting until I met Betty. Now I have Betty, her mom, Andrew, and, most nights, Stephen and Margaret at my house. We are one big happy family. I need to get out of here for a while!"

Linda said, "Harry, I have the perfect escape. You, Daniel, Ralph, and I will take a road trip to check out wedding and honeymoon venues."

"Perfect, but I don't know jack about weddings."

"Don't worry, Harry. This time, you are the one coming along for the ride. You can negotiate the prices after I ascertain the costs. This is going to be the wedding of the year. You will see."

"We'll go to all of our favorite places en route to Santa Barbara."

Harry put in a call to Betty to tell her the plan.

"Oh, Harry, I'll go with you."

Harry reassured her he could handle this and would be back in a week or so. He needed her at the office to keep an eye on things. Harry went home to pick up the suitcase Andrew had packed for him.

Once he was back in the car, he asked, "Who is driving, Ralph? Me or you?"

Ralph said, "Sit back, boss, and relax. Leave the driving to me."

Harry sat in the back seat singing "Hotel California," and his friends chimed in. They hadn't sung together in months. So much had changed. This was just what he needed, riding down the road and singing with his friends.

Linda said, "Harry, you seem unhappy. With everything you have in your life, you are so blessed. What's wrong?"

Harry was pensive. "Linda, after all the chaos and craziness we went through, you'd think I would appreciate the calm. I used to be quite content, and then Betty came into my life, and it turned upside down in a wonderful way. Now, I am back to dealing with traffic going to the office, spending time helping other businesses with their security needs. I guess it is the 'let-down after the big game' feeling. Maybe I just need to get away."

The scenery changed, and the ocean came into view. Harry remembered the adventures he and his new friends had up and down the coast. What he remembered the most was when he'd wanted Betty to be there with him. Before he finished his thought, Linda had her on the phone.

"Betty's on the phone, Harry."

"Linda, how do you do that?"

"Harry, from the beginning, I told you I know everything about you."

Betty said, "Harry, I am happy you called. I'll meet you tonight."

Harry sat back and smiled. "Life's been good to me so far."

After picking Betty up at the Santa Barbara airport, they drove to the Ritz-Carlton Bacara, an exclusive five-star hotel. The events manager, Barbara, greeted them in the lobby and began to show them around.

"The ballroom will hold two hundred and fifty people. How many will be attending?"

Betty was looking around, counting the exits.

Barbara said, "Please explain why the exits are so important. Is everything okay, Betty? Would you like to see the table settings and menus?"

Betty laughed. "Oh, yes, of course." She was considering if this room would be perfect for her mother's wedding and private enough for the FBI who's who guest list that would be attending. Betty took out her phone and called Gloria. "Okay, Mom, look at this." She panned the room and showed Gloria the view, including the patio. When they were outside, she whispered, "It is very private and has ten exits."

Barbara showed Harry and Betty to their suite. "I'll meet you downstairs at noon to do a tasting. Will you be picking the menu yourself, or will your mother be coming down to choose the food?"

"No, she trusts our judgment," Betty said. "See you at noon."

The door to the suite closed, and Harry turned to Betty. "We have two hours. Do you know what we can do to fill those?"

Betty smiled and said, "Yes, join me in the tub."

Before Harry and Betty left for the meeting, they called house-keeping to repair their suite. Harry left fifty dollars on the pillow. They met Barbara in the ballroom and saw an assortment of table decorations. The food and wine tastings were served, and they chose a pear salad, crab legs, filet mignon, asparagus, and red potatoes with accompanying pairings of California wines.

Harry negotiated the prices based on Linda's figures. Before long, Barbara was agreeing to everything he wanted, and the hotel threw in two free suites. He took out his phone and contacted Linda, who was sitting at her desk, dressed in a blue suit.

She smiled and told Barbara, "It's a pleasure doing business with you. A deposit check will be in the mail in the morning." Linda whispered in Harry's ear, "Good job, Harry. You and Betty go have some fun."

BLESSED EVENT

The day before the wedding, Gloria, Andrew, Betty, and Harry arrived at the hotel and went to their rooms. Gloria and Betty were in one suite, and Harry and Andrew in the other.

The next day, guests were arriving. Never were there so many men at a wedding packing a gun.

Gloria's past was filled with powerful men, FBI agents, and heads of governments. Included among the guests were Harry's parents and his aunts and uncles, many who had not met Betty. This was going to be their opportunity. They had planned a small family reunion the day after the wedding so everyone could get to know each other.

Abbe and Sara Mendelbaum wished it were Harry and Betty's wedding they were attending. Abbe went toward Harry's room to spend some private time with his son. He met Stephen in the hallway.

Stephen and Abbe hugged, and Abbe said, "We haven't seen you in years. Stephen, you are looking good. I hear you are working with Harry now. All the boys are coming back together."

"Not that schmuck, Rudnick!"

"Stephen, that was such a *shanda*. He was such a nice boy."

They went into the suite to find Harry and Andrew getting dressed and putting on their boutonnieres. Abbe walked up to his son. "So, Harry, when will you and Betty being tying the knot? We started having children when we were your age, and we want to be grandparents before we get too old."

"Pop, relax! We won't make you wait too long. Just enjoy yourself. We will all get together tomorrow."

The Mendelbaums' family rabbi was standing in the front of the room. The *chuppa* had been set up. The guests were being seated. The FBI was seated on the right, and the family was seated on the left. The visiting English diplomats who came for the wedding sat with the family up front next to Harry and Betty.

Once Gloria arrived at the *chuppa*, Andrew was there to meet her. The rabbi offered words of welcome and a prayer. "The

One who is mighty and blessed, above all, please bless Andrew and Gloria."

Andrew and Gloria stared deeply into each other's eyes, lost in the moment. Time stood still for lovers' bliss. They exchanged rings, and the rabbi placed a glass in a napkin. He asked Andrew to perform the breaking of the glass, and he shattered it into a thousand pieces. He embraced Gloria and kissed her. The whole family and their friends were cheering: *"Mazel tov!"*

The receiving line was formed. Ted Herman's big band started playing the first dance for Andrew and Gloria. After a few moments, they were joined by Betty and Harry, the Mendelbaums, the Kaplans, the Greenbergs, the Levis, and FBI men with their wives or girlfriends.

Prudence, elegantly dressed, was dancing with her new friend, James, the head of the FBI. He was still a little tender from last night, but he didn't want to miss the opportunity to hold Prudence close.

A waiter tried to sell a gram of cocaine to an intoxicated undercover agent. He was quickly detained by fifteen officers and taken into custody. Since no one wanted to leave this glorious wedding celebration, they handcuffed the young man to the ice cream freezer in the kitchen.

Stephen, ever wanting to be helpful, went to see if he needed legal representation. The young man, who was sweating profusely, said, "I guess so. I don't think I can afford you."

Stephen said, "Well, we will see what happens. I will check back with you at the end of the night."

The band played on. The time came to do the Israeli folk dance called the *hora*, where everyone danced in a circle to the song "Hava Nagila." Stephen was first in line.

The dance started out slow and went faster and faster. Someone usually went in the middle of the circle and did the *kazatsky*. Stephen stepped into the circle, and to everyone's amazement, he could crouch down, kick out, and balance on one foot. He continued on until he was exhausted, and he pulled in an agent to take his place.

It was quite funny to see the FBI agent trying to do the *kazatsky*. He tried hard and even split his pants. He was no match for Stephen. There was so much laughter.

During the excitement, the drugs seemed to have vanished, and late that night, the waiter was set free for lack of evidence. Even though the FBI didn't charge him, he was fired by hotel management and escorted out of the building.

Stephen told him, "Nothing I can do about that one."

Gloria and Andrew's wedding and reception was more than they could have imagined. They toasted Linda and Harry.

Since Linda couldn't be there in person, they held up Harry's tablet and showed her on the screen. She was wearing a stunning midnight-blue gown.

She waved and blessed the couple as they toasted her. Harry was beaming, knowing he and Linda created this union. He wished the couple much happiness.

Questions started circling about who that beautiful woman was. If she was so important, why wasn't she there in person? Rumors flew until one of the FBI agents said, "I know who she is. I saw the story in the *Hollywood Reporter*. She's the mystery woman who was dating Daniel Craig when they were in Paris. She's a knockout."

As Linda continued her conversation with Gloria, someone wrapped a hand around her waist and over her shoulder. Everyone gasped because it was Daniel Craig caressing her.

Daniel said, "Hi, Harry! You throw a great party! If I hadn't whisked Linda back off to Paris, she would have been there. Sorry! I think she would have invited me as her plus one."

Over Linda's other shoulder, a very handsome man dressed in a dark suit with a cap, as though he was their driver, appeared. "Hi, Harry. I look forward to seeing you soon." He winked.

"We are off to Menton," Linda said. The three each threw a kiss, and the screen went black.

Gloria and Andrew, ready to consummate their union as a married couple, gathered their paperwork and headed off to their room as people threw birdseed at them. After they left the ballroom, the guests continued dancing and drinking until two in the morning.

Gloria and Andrew reached the door of their suite.

Andrew said, "This may not be your first marriage, but it will be the best!" He picked her up in his arms and carried her over the threshold.

Meanwhile, back in the ballroom dancing to the music, Harry and Betty went onto the patio to look at the night sky. They stood there staring up at the stars, talking about the constellations and smelling the scent of evening star jasmine.

Betty turned around to kiss Harry, but he was on his knees. "Harry, what are you doing? We can't do that here."

He laughed. "Oh, Betty, you know how to ruin the moment."

"What do you mean, Harry?"

"Come on, Betty. This is serious."

Betty had had quite a bit to drink and was feeling very silly, and she started to laugh. "Okay, Harry. I will behave."

Harry looked up at Betty and put out his hand. "Betty, may I have your hand in marriage?" He held out a beautiful diamond engagement ring. "Will you marry me?"

She took his hand to help him up and kissed him. "Oh, Harry, are you asking me today so you can tell your family tomorrow that you are engaged? You stinker."

"No! I didn't think of that, but now that you mention it, why not? We can tell them at breakfast."

"I love you, Harry."

"I love you, Betty. Let's get to our room and seal the deal."

REUNION

In the morning, both couples had headaches and were nursing hangovers. Four Bloody Marys were carried down the hallway, two delivered to each suite.

Harry told Betty, "My parents are always early. We need to get ready. My father said he was bringing the Teitelbaums, whom we forgot to invite." Harry shook his head.

"Have I met them?"

"No, they hang out with my parents, but they are always on the go. I don't see them much either. You'll like them. They are pretty funny."

Harry and Betty met Gloria and Andrew in the elevator on their way, and Gloria said, "Do you really want me at your family reunion? I'm not really part of your family."

Harry smiled. "Gloria, this is your weekend. Since yesterday, you are part of my family. Well, you soon will be."

Gloria caught the remark and said, "Harry, is there something going on that I don't know?"

"Keep your hair on, sweetie. You'll find out soon."

The banter put them in a good mood, the headaches subsiding, and they were ready to face the music.

———

The Mendelbaums and the Levis were already seated, waiting for the food to be served. Harry and Betty appeared, along with Gloria and Andrew. They all stood up and cheered, "*Mazel tov.*"

Abbe and Sara were excited to see Harry and Betty and meet Betty's family. Harry took Betty to each table to meet every one of his family members present.

When they finally sat down to eat, Harry said, "Okay! Okay! There is something I need to tell you all. Last night, I asked Betty to marry me, and she said yes."

Another cheer of *mazel tov* was expressed, and everyone started eating. Gloria ran over to Betty and Harry and hugged them. "I am so excited, Betty. Who knew we would both be so happy?"

Abbe and Sara said, "We hope you want to have children."

"Mom, please! Give us a chance to plan our wedding first. Can you two just relax?"

"I have never relaxed in my life," Abbe said. "What are you talking about? Ranching, traveling, working hard, and just dealing with your mother's crazy uncle has been a full-time job. Thank God you are not like him."

Harry looked at his pop. "Really?"

"You know what I mean."

"Pop, there are some family stories better left untold. Would you be okay with me giving Andrew and Gloria some of the land? I know Betty would like to keep her mom close to us. That would be a perfect place for us to build vacation homes. Of course, there will be a suite of rooms for you and Mom to come and visit."

"Harry, I would be honored to have you and your family live on the land. That was always my dream. It has been in our family for over a hundred and fifty years."

"I thought you would say that, but I wanted to ask you first." Harry turned to the newly married couple. "A toast to the bride and groom. I would like to present my gift to you. Gloria and Andrew, please come forward."

Gloria and Andrew looked at each other, and Gloria pinched him. "What is up his sleeve this time?"

As they approached Harry, he held out a letter gifting them with fifty prime acres of land in Montana.

"This was our family ranch, and we want to welcome you to the family. We can both build houses near each other, and you'll be able to spend lots of time with your grandchildren when they show up."

Gloria took the letter, folded it, and put it in her purse. She couldn't imagine a better way to start the rest of her life with Andrew, Betty, Harry, Stephen, Margaret, Stanley, and the crew.

After breakfast, Harry and Betty headed out the front door toward the valet parking.

"Betty," Harry said. "I have one more surprise for you! Now close your eyes and hold my hand." He had the valet bring up the new car he purchased for Betty. "You may open your eyes!"

When Betty opened her eyes, she spotted a 2021 pastel-yellow Bentley convertible with a huge red bow on the hood. Betty put her arms around Harry's neck and kissed him. They jumped into the Bentley.

Ralph drove the car away from the hotel. Linda and Daniel were on the screen watching Betty and Harry cuddle in the back seat. They drove off into the sunset singing.

This was not the end of our story.

fini

ABOUT THE AUTHORS

Robert & Carol Teitelbaum

Robert John Teitelbaum, Author, Publisher, Actor, Casting Director, and Rare Coin expert. Teitelbaum Publishing offers Authors personal services from editing, to cover art, programing, placement, and social media promotion. Robert's vast experience brings expertise in many areas to his clients.

Carol Teitelbaum, LMFT is a licensed Psychotherapist in Rancho Mirage. She began her career in 1985 and still works full time. Her knowledge of human behaviors and personalities added richness to the characters.

Carol and Robert have been married fifty-eight years.

9 781736 367568